a hongkong story

My City

a hongkong story

by

XI XI

Translated by Eva Hung

Illustrations by Xi Xi

— An Authorized Translation —

A *RENDITIONS* Paperback

© The Chinese University of Hong Kong 1993
All Rights Reserved. ISBN 962-7255-11-4

Renditions Paperbacks
are published by
The Research Centre for Translation
The Chinese University of Hong Kong

General Editors
Eva Hung   T.L. Tsim

Printed in Hong Kong

I decided to write a lively novel, to write about the younger generation — their lives and their city — to feel the way they feel, to speak in the language they use. When the novel was serialized, I came across a literary policeman in the street who said to me: I have absolutely no idea what it means. I was delighted .... Later I heard about another literary policeman's comment: my strolling has gone completely off key. I was even more delighted.

— Xi Xi, Preface to the 1989 Yunchen edition

Translator's Introduction

About the Author

Xi Xi 西西 (pronounced "See See") is the pen-name of Zhang Yan 張彦. Of Cantonese extraction, Xi Xi was born in Shanghai in 1938 and received her primary education there. Like so many Hong Kong people of her generation, she escaped to Hong Kong with her family in 1950 from China shortly after the communist take-over. Having arrived in the territory as a child, she is among the first generation of writers to have been educated and nurtured in Hong Kong. Xi Xi graduated from the Grantham College of Education in 1958 and became a primary school teacher. It was during the 1960s that she first established a local literary reputation — as a poet, fiction writer, script writer, and film and art critic.

Though Xi Xi has used a number of pen-names in her career as a writer, from the mid-1970s onwards she has published most of her fiction under the name Xi Xi, and all her collected works are also published under this name. The word *xi* 西 literally means "west", but Zhang Yan's choice of this word as her pen-name has little to do with the word's meaning; rather, it is treated as a pictograph. The following is Xi Xi's own explanation of her pen-name:

> When I was young I loved playing a game similar to hopscotch, which we called "Building Houses" or "Aeroplane Hopping". First you draw a series of squares on the ground. Then you tie a

string of paper clips into a knot and toss it into one of the squares. You then hop from square to square until you reach the one with the knot in it, pick the knot up and hop your way back to where you started .... The Chinese word *xi* looks like a girl in a skirt with her two feet planted in a square. Put two of them side by side, and they are like two frames of a film, a girl in a skirt playing hopscotch in two squares.[1]

As Stephen Soong suggests in his article on Xi Xi,[2] this pen-name reveals that the author has retained a childlike joy in her perception and depiction of life. Critics have pointed out that Xi Xi often adopts extraordinary narrative angles in her fictional work, a characteristic which can probably be attributed to the freshness of her childlike vision. In this respect, *My City* is perhaps the most representative of Xi Xi's fictional works.

Xi Xi has expressed on a number of occasions her admiration for the works of Latin American writers. With Gabriel Garcia Marquez's winning of the Nobel Prize for literature, magic realism swept the world like a whirlwind in the 1980s. In the case of Xi Xi, literary contact with magic realism started in the early 1970s when she first read the works of Mario Vargas Llosa and Marquez. In her own words, these writers' approaches to literature opened up new horizons for her: "it was as if the world was again a lovely garden full of fragrant flowers and fruit."[3] *My City* was written in this joyous spirit. It is perhaps the best kind of literary influence — not a copy, not a transplant, but a rejuvenation of the zeal for life and creativity.

Though Xi Xi won a number of literary prizes in Hong Kong in the 1960s and 1970s, and was one of the editors of two major Hong Kong

---

[1] Translation adapted from "Building a House: Introducing Xi Xi" by Stephen Soong, translated by Kwok-kan Tam, *A Girl Like Me and Other Stories* (Hong Kong: Renditions Paperbacks, 1986) p.84.
[2] Ibid. pp. 83-89.
[3] Xi Xi's preface to the 1989 Taipei Yunchen edition of *My City*.

literary journals, her name only became widely known after she was awarded Taiwan's prestigious *United Daily* prize for fiction in 1983. In the mid-1980s Xi Xi gave up her teaching career to become a full-time writer, thus occupying a unique position among serious writers in Hong Kong. In the last three decades, Xi Xi has been one of the territory's most prolific writers, a fact which is partially concealed by her use of different pen-names and the variety of genres she covers — she is equally at home in poetry, fiction, the occasional essay, translation, film review and art criticism, and has published extensively in magazines and newspapers in Hong Kong and Taiwan.[4] She is also the editor of a contemporary fiction series authored by mainland writers and published in Taiwan.

About the Story

When *My City*, Xi Xi's first novel, was serialized in the literary supplement of the *Hong Kong Express*快報from January to June, 1975, the pen-name Zhang Yan used for it was Ah Guo阿果, or Fruits. In this sense we can say that *My City* is Fruits' novel. Fruits is of course the main character of the novel, and he shares with the author a great zest for life, but there is a difference between him and the narrator, just as there is a difference between the narrator and the author. We can say that Xi Xi has projected various facets of her personality and vision onto most of the characters in this novel; if Fruits seems to have been allocated a larger share, it is perhaps only because he features more prominently in the novel. At the same time, however, all the characters are prototypes representing the territory's past, present and future. Though *My City* was meant to capture the spirit of the present, the past is an integral part of the story, for it is only through juxtaposition that the reader is made aware of how the generation of Fruits and his friends — the fortunate generation — differs from that of his mother Grace and the old carpenter North.

---

[4] For a comprehensive list of Xi Xi's publications from 1955 to 1990, see Gan Yuzhen 甘玉珍 and Guan Xiuqiong關秀瓊, "Chronology of Xi Xi's Works" 西西作品編年表, *Bafang wenyi congkan* 八方文藝叢刊Vol. 12, November 1990, pp.105-154.

Readers unfamiliar with the history of China or that of Hong Kong may find some references puzzling. In the novel there are scenes describing the influx of refugees from China during the Cultural Revolution of 1966 to 1976 (Chapter 14) and references to the beginning of the Vietnamese boat-people problem (Chapter 14), but there are also far less obvious references to the Anti-Japanese war, World War II, Hong Kong under Japanese occupation (Chapter 13), and the tides of refugees coming from China after the Communist take-over in 1949 (Chapter 13). To quote just two examples: the brief mention of North's friend, the poet-apprentice, who left Hong Kong to "guard an abstract door" (Chapter 7) is a reference to the thousands of young men who returned to China to fight the Japanese during World War II; the little girl with a piece of cloth sewn to her clothes and the girl's mother represent the millions of refugees and what they went through during the Anti-Japanese war and the Chinese civil war. An incident of more topical relevance is the departure of the water-lilies, who were no doubt among the tide of emigrants leaving Hong Kong in the late-1960s to mid-1970s to escape from a city politically threatened by mainland China.

The translator is thus faced with the problem of whether to provide annotation or not. I have decided against annotation for two reasons. First, *My City* is basically a novel of fun, and heavy annotation will only turn it into a haphazard information manual. Second, even Hong Kong readers of Fruits' generation cannot be certain that they recognize all the historical and geographical references in this novel, so no annotation can be complete. I hope that by providing relevant background information in the introduction, I can make the author's approach sufficiently clear to the readers of this translation. After all, Xi Xi's story-telling technique is strong enough to stand on its own.

Though seemingly completely contemporary, *My City* is steeped in traditional family relationships the richness of which cannot be fully savoured in one or two readings. One example will show how hidden elements may gradually come to the surface. In Chapter 1 we are told that the water-lilies give Fruits and his family the free use of a huge house left

to the women by their late father. We are then told that the water-lilies
occupy a prominent position in the funeral of Fruits' father — they are
his sisters. Yet throughout the novel there is little to show that Fruits
regards the women as his relatives, nor does he refer to them and their
father in kinship terms. Later on in the novel we are told that the
water-lilies and their father had lived in the mansion before the war, but
there is no mention of Fruits' father. Had there been a falling out in the
family? We are not told. Then the most obvious explanation suddenly
stared me in the face: could it be that Fruits' father, as an illegitimate child
and half-brother of the water-lilies, was never considered part of the
family? After nearly four years of reading and translating *My City*, I am
still on a journey of discovery.

On Narrative Techniques

Critics have pointed out the similarity of the narrative technique in
My City to the famous Song dynasty Chinese scroll painting "A Trip
Upstream on Qingming Festival" 清明河上圖.[5] The proposal that a new
set of aesthetics should be adopted to judge a novel is indicative of how
My City differs from the traditional concept of what a novel is, or should
be.[6] Readers familiar with Chinese painting techniques would recognize
in *My City* effects very similar to those of a "scattered perspective"散點
透視— instead of one focal point or one point of observation, different
objects in a painting are shown from different perspectives — a technique
not dissimilar to that adopted by the Cubists. The analogy with "A Trip
Upstream on Qingming Festival" is therefore not only valid in the sense
that both the painting and the novel are depictions of a particular city
at a moment in history, but also because many of the techniques used

---

[5] The critic who first proposed this analogy is He Furen 何福仁. His article "One Way
of Reading *My City*" is included in the Taipei Yunchen edition of the novel.

[6] William Tay recalls in his article "Random Thoughts on Reading Xi Xi's Fiction"
(*Bafang* Vol. 12, November, 1990, pp. 95-97) that even in 1988 some Taiwan adjudicators
for literary prizes were still making comments such as "this is not the way to write fiction".

in the depiction are comparable to one another.

While we are on the subject of analogies with art, I would like to suggest that there exists another possible analogue — a western one — for what Xi Xi tries to accomplish in *My City*. The paintings of Canaletto (1697-1768), the Venetian Renaissance artist whose works depicting the scenes of his native city won him wide recognition and international fame in the twentieth century, are a different but similarly effective analogue for *My City*. Xi Xi's first novel shares with Canaletto's paintings a colourful brilliance and a sense of joy which verges on exuberance (while colours in "A Trip Upstream on Qingming Festival" are much subtler). Moreover, art historians have discovered that Caneletto's depictions of Venetian scenes are not always straight-forward copies of reality: palaces and other architectural structures are often transferred from one site to another on canvas, creating a Venice which is familiar and yet different from the actual eighteenth century city. Similarly, Xi Xi's depiction of Hong Kong in *My City* is a creative artist's impression of aspects of life in the territory. It is perhaps for this reason that the novel is, aptly, entitled *My City* rather than *Our City*.

In her preface to the 1989 edition of *My City*, Xi Xi makes a special mention of the painters Henri Matisse (1869-1954), Joan Mirò (1893-1983) and Marc Chagall (1889-1986). It is thus not accidental that some sections of the novel give the distinct impression of being fantastic scenes from Fauvist and Surrealist paintings. In reading these sections, I am particularly reminded of Mirò's childlike dreamscapes and his depiction of birds and stars. These sections also call to mind what André Breton says in the *Surrealist Manifesto* about the power of imagination being a source of eternal youth — not an inaccurate description of Xi Xi's artistic vision in *My City*.

One Reader's Experience

When I first read *My City* in 1979, I did not get beyond Chapter 3. Being something of a blue-stocking, and having started writing creatively myself, I found Xi Xi's "self-indulgent rambling" and her "pollution" of the Chinese language impossible to accept. I turned to the novel again in 1989, shortly after I finished translating Gu Cheng's fantasia of a poetry cycle — *The Bulin File*.[7] This second attempt at reading *My City* produced a dramatically different impression — I was hypnotized by the richness of the novel's linguistic and technical innovations, by the sense of sheer fun, but most importantly by the author's depth of feeling about Hong Kong. It is perhaps a cliché to say that an author has managed to put into words one's own innermost thoughts and feelings, but for two generations of Hong Kong people — those similar in age to Liberty, Fruits, Braids and other young characters in the novel — Xi Xi has done just that.

There are of course those who dislike *My City*: the same qualities which fascinate some irritate others. Having been on both sides of the fence, I understand that this is not a novel which appeals to everyone. Linguistic purists and "literary policemen": you have been warned.

About the Translation

It is this translator's belief that all translations are but specific interpretations of the original work. If the original is a natural landscape, what the readers of the translation get is the landscape on film, seen through the eyes of the person who manipulates the camera, i.e., the translator.[8] The natural landscape is of course filmed from the best possible angle under prevalent objective circumstances, but this should not obscure the fact that the celluloid landscape presents only certain facets of the real thing, and that there are many more possible angles of looking at the natural landscape. In the translation of a work like *My City*, the translator is reminded constantly of the subtle — sometimes

---

[7] Collected in Gu Cheng, *Selected Poems* (Hong Kong: Renditions Paperbacks, 1990).

[8] It is of course equally valid to say that a work of literature is a celluloid landscape — life being the natural landscape. If we pursue this metaphor, the process of translation is one in which we try to produce a new celluloid landscape resembling as closely as possible the one produced by the author.

even obvious — differences between the real landscape and the celluloid one. I therefore feel compelled to explain my approach towards translating *My City* and the various tactics I have used to achieve my chosen purposes.

Many of the difficulties I encountered in the process of translation are direct results of differences between the Chinese and English languages. The first and most obvious obstacle I had to overcome was that of tenses: Chinese verbs do not denote tenses and are as a result capable of suggesting an eternal present. With English, one has to make a hard choice. There is no denying the fact that the insertion of tense differences affects the flow of the narrative — seamless transitions in the original become much more clearly marked boundaries in this English version. It would have been easier to opt for a past-tense narrative, but given Xi Xi's clear intention of capturing the here and now when she wrote the novel, the choice of the simple present seems justified. Nevertheless, throughout the preparation of the first draft, I had misgivings about the effect of this decision, and some chapters were actually changed two or three times as experiments in tenses. Ultimately, whatever tense one chooses for the narrative is only a compromise, a fact that Chinese-English translators have to accept most of the time.

There is also the problem of the use of dialect in the original. Hong Kong is basically a Cantonese-speaking community, and in her attempts to capture a strong local flavour, Xi Xi made liberal use of Cantonese vocabulary and syntax, a decision which was decried during the novel's serialization, but which she has stuck to despite some harsh comments, rightly asserting that otherwise the novel would be turned into "someone else's city" or "some other city".

As all translators are aware, dialects are one of the most tricky problems in literary translation. In the case of *My City* the problems are compounded because dialectal elements are not confined to dialogue, but are also sprinkled liberally all over the narrative and placed right next to literary allusions and mock-formal language. Since I am not capable of adopting a particular English dialect as a "linguistic equivalent" of

Cantonese, nor do I believe in such a solution, I had to use different tactics to achieve a comparable, but not necessarily similar, effect.

For me, the choice of British English for translation is Hobson's choice, since that is the kind of English I grew up with, but the occasional use of Americanisms is deliberate and aim at achieving two purposes: first, to reflect actual conditions in the linguistic melting-pot that is Hong Kong; second, in the hope to jar on my reader's ears, just as Xi Xi's use of certain Cantonese words and syntax jars on the ears of some Chinese readers. (American readers will probably have an impression of *My City* which is closer to that of native Chinese readers of the original, for the simple reason that they will take more note of British usage.) There are also cases where I choose to follow specifically Hong Kong usage. I have also attempted to produce some deliberately awkward — though hopefully not overly awkward — sentences, with similar results in mind.

The biggest problem for the translator of *My City* is Xi Xi's keenness for word-play. The mention of Hong Kong place names in slightly disguised form is one element in this network of linguistic fun. Xi Xi's decision to play with Hong Kong place names is probably a means of making readers look at familiar places from a new point of view, but it also serves another purpose — *My City* in a way represents city life in many growing metropolises. Though the novel is set in Hong Kong, the events in the novel can take place in many other cities; hence the advantage of disguising local place names. In view of this I have only provided a limited number of footnotes identifying some local landmarks in the early chapters, but have otherwise followed Xi Xi's method: those familiar with Hong Kong will recognize the disguised names without much difficulty.

The same cannot be said of place names which are used as part of a pun. In cases when a word serves two functions, the translator frequently has to opt for one, and in this novel I have invariably opted for the pun. After all, the spirit of fun is much more important than geographical accuracy.

The network of linguistic fun also includes many puns unrelated to place names, topical and literary allusions, as well as nursery rhymes and children's songs. On average there is one instance of word-play to every two pages of *My City*. Translating such a novel would have been impossible had it not been for one thing — over the last hundred years, Hong Kong has become internationalized to such an extent that the Cantonese language in Hong Kong reflects extensive foreign influence. One very good example is the Cantonese word "pineapple" used to denote home-made bombs. The term originated in English and was at first used to denote hand grenades. Such cross-culture borrowings are the basis for my decision to use as little annotation as possible.

Many of the children's songs mentioned in *My City* are based on European melodies. These songs have become so much a part of the Hong Kong Cantonese tradition that very few Hong Kong people are aware of their foreign origin. Thus, instead of reverting to the original European lyrics, I have translated the Chinese lyrics into an English version which fits in with the melodies. There is, however, less methodical consistency in the translation of Chinese nursery rhymes: some are translated, while others are replaced with comparable English versions: the decision depends entirely on the context. In one particular case I have even introduced an echo of T.S. Eliot's "The Hollow Men" — in a spirit which I think the author would approve of. As readers will notice, Xi Xi herself is not shy of literary allusions. One of the most frequently mentioned examples is the line "one was a guava tree, the other was not a guava tree" (p. 3), a direct quote from an occasional essay by Lu Xun (1881- 1936). References to western works of literature are of course much more easily recognizable. Since readers of the original are given the pleasure of discovering for themselves the various levels of language used, I have decided to provide essential background information in this introduction, rather than in the form of footnotes.

Acknowledgements

I have incurred many debts of gratitude in the last two years during which this English translation of *My City* slowly took shape. First and foremost, I am grateful to Xi Xi for entrusting me with her novel in the full knowledge (since she herself is also a literary translator) that I will not be able to produce anything near a perfect rendition, and also for her help in supplying information which was unavailable to me. In terms of debts as a translator, I owe most to David Pollard whose knowledge of "gubbins" used in diverse walks of life saved me from making a large number of embarrassing mistakes. I would also like to thank Janice Wickeri, Oliver Stunt and Chu Chiyu, who went over my drafts with meticulous care. Needless to say, I am solely responsible for the mistakes and idiosyncrasies which remain in this translation. Conversations with Lai Suk-yee were extremely helpful in clarifying my ideas about art analogies with *My City*. I am grateful to Cecilia Ip for a superb production job, to Elaine Wong for her help in researching botanical and geographical names, and to Heung Lai-wan who gave me the inspiration to solve the translation problems related to a riddle (p. 120). Last but not least, I would like to thank Wong Kai-chee, who sent me much useful material on Xi Xi's works, and whose preference for *My City* among all of Xi Xi's fictional work reinforced my own bias in favour of the novel. It was a bias which stood me in good stead during my moments of doubt about the wisdom of undertaking this most difficult translation task.

E.H.
10 July, 1993

1

I nod my head to them. Well, except for nodding my head, what can I say? This old and fascinating mansion with its seventeen doors — they have just said: You can live here.

By "you" they mean my mother Grace, my sister Braids and me, Fruits. As for them, two are my father's younger sisters, the other one is his older sister. Yesterday, early in the morning, I thought hard for a full two hours before I recalled having met them twice before. Once, I recalled, they looked like water-lilies, that is to say, brilliant. The other time, I recalled, they looked like lotus roots, their faces grey and muddy.

Today, they have come to find me.

— No swimming

they said. They thought they were kings. They told me to go with them to take a look at the house, and I did. I saw the house: it and its house-friends queued up in a way that pleased themselves, lining both sides of the road; they looked like a forest. The mansion stands at a corner, slightly away from the road. While other houses are tall, it is short; while other houses are slim, it is plump; while other houses are lively and happy, it is dull and stupid. That reminds me: it is exactly like me, Fruits. It was sleeping, so I let it sleep on. The weather wasn't cold, but it hugged itself tightly. The grey stone wall wrapped around it like an extra-thick woollen cardigan, and on top of that was a spotted woollen scarf, *and* gloves, *and* socks.

There's an iron gate on the ground floor, guarded by five padlocks. Behind the iron gate is the main door with a spring lock. Behind the door is the staircase where five of me can squeeze onto a single step.

— The first floor, you can live there
— The ground floor, that's for Old North, the doorman

the water-lilies said. They also said they didn't know how many years it'd be before they'd come back, that perhaps they wouldn't come back at all. It's too much bother, and too degrading, for them to look back to this nest, which is like ninth grade *longjing* tea in the chrysanthemum season. Having said all this, they raised their eyebrows and fluffed up the clusters of pink ostrich feathers blooming on their shoulders. Today, they looked completely like water-lilies.

We went up the stairs together. The wooden steps echoed under our feet — plom, plom. Some ploms were light, followed by one or two heavy ones. It was a kind of rhythm, stressed, and unstressed. My mind was suddenly filled with stories. Plom plom. I thought: I'm really in a forest; the barefoot head-hunters are drumming. Plom plom. Then I thought: I've come across a huge church organ. If there's a group of us we can skip and jump on the stairs and play out a tune, something like: Bake some bread, bake some bread, it sure tastes good.[1] But the water-lilies would not have liked that kind of song, I'm sure. The water-lilies don't like walking; with a wave of the hand, they told me to take a look around on my own, to get to know the house's rooms, walls, doors, windows, and tables, desks, chairs, and bowls, buckets, basins, and head and shoulders, knees and toes, and "a" for apple "b" for boy, "c" for cat and "d" for dog. And so I went to look at the ceilings and the staircase landing on my own, and walked through I don't know how many doors.

I met a large number of doors. The biggest one, which has two leaves

---

[1] The original lyrics go as follows:
    Pat-a-cake, pat-a-cake, baker's man
    Bake me a cake as fast as you can
    Pat it and prick it and mark it with "B"
    And there will be plenty for baby and me

closing toward the centre, was dark, like black dates. When I first met it it was closed, just as I have described it, standing there proudly. I pushed hard, and it conceded a gap through which ten cats could squeeze — sq—ueak

it cried, trailing the last syllable. It also threw bread-crumb-like or washing-flakes-like dust on my head. I sneezed twice because of that; I thought it was snowing. Later, I met the windows. On the window panes there were layers of waves in relief, some sort of ancient script written on tortoise shells. From this side of the window one could not see the colours and shapes on the other side; neither could the scenery on the other side get through to this side. Only sunlight could get through, but when it did its brightness was not the same. I studied the sunlight for a good while and discovered what it was like: Grand's oatmeal.

Later, by the crack of a door festooned with clumps of dust, I met a stubby bathtub heavily stained with rust and I very politely wished it a good afternoon. After that I met an arched door (the shape of which is like the cross section of a loaf of bread). Beyond the arched door was a corridor (which would have looked marvellous had there been a Turkish rug on its wall). At the end of the corridor was an open bridgeway (a bridgeway is a hanging road). Underneath the bridgeway was a skywell (a skywell is an open courtyard). There were trees in the skywell (one was a guava tree, the other was not a guava tree). The tree branches meticulously cut out patterns traced out by the sunlight with the intention of pasting them onto the noses of the patterned tiles in the courtyard (the fragrance of guava blossoms would stay in the nose).

Later, I met birds, all of them sparrows, engaged in a hopping competition at the edge of the water tank cover on the roof. Occasionally they stretched their wings, and in so doing, they merged with the spotted bamboo clothes poles and the big, striped, coarse flower pots, thus rearranging the colour scheme.

And so I nodded my head to the water-lilies.

— Go back and tell your mother

the water-lilies said.

Mother says nothing.

It is a Sunday. Sunday is just like any other day in the week: as a rule, various things happen, some novel, some extremely ancient. This day something ancient is taking place. In the early morning, Mother's eyes were already as red as tomatoes and swollen to the size of pumpkins. Seven or eight women are now standing around her, extending from various directions their plump or thin, long or short, right or left but equally white hands to support her. They're all wearing black robes, that's why their hands look white. However, one or two hands boast nail colours of an attractive red. Besides having extraordinarily eye-catching hands, this black-robed group share another characteristic — each and every one of them show a distinctive and easily recognizable face and head.

Normally these heads and faces like to hide in the photo album at home. When it was new the album was flat; now it has almost turned into an American football. If you're careless when you take it out, a pile of faces will fall out of it: some of the faces used to appear on the evening of the cake-eating festival in the company of the round moon;[2] others appeared in the grand swap of oranges, wine bottles, candy boxes and sweet things during Chinese New Year, standing behind red envelopes. Today they have broken with custom and have turned up together, and they're wearing the same ill-fitting though rather becoming black robes. They all flaunt their suddenly eye-catching hands in front of and behind Mother, and are all acting so solicitously.

Facing me stands another row of black robes. On top of the black cloth-tents are three strange faces, all looking like lotus roots. One face (sympathetic mode) is diligently explicating the feelings behind the face, which means its eyes are shut and its left and right eyebrows are drawn close together. Another face (sorrowful mode) is ventilating air with either its mouth or its nose, it's hard to tell exactly. Yet another face (sad and helpless mode) reveals only two red ears; all other facial features, including spectacles, are neatly covered by a blue handkerchief with a

---

[2]The Mid-autumn Festival.

white floral pattern. By the side of these three faces, slightly apart from them, stands my aunt Liberty all by herself. As I look more closely, I realize that my sister Braids is standing beside her. My aunt Liberty's posture is like that of a depressed scarecrow standing on a rock. Her mouth is shut, tightly shut. My sister Braids is holding onto one end of her long robe, her head buried in its folds. Occasionally she shows her temple and her neck, like a squirrel. The tissue paper in her hands has turned into bits of cotton wool, which she presses on her mouth, and after a while, on her nose.

I'm standing alone beside some thick ropes. The ropes were originally lying motionless behind my heels, but someone in front of me suddenly gave them a tug, and they hurriedly started swimming away like water snakes. There are many more people standing in front of me. One of them, a big fellow, looks like a commander; maybe he had been a lieutenant during the war (gesticulating mode); he is giving orders. Try as I may, I cannot remember this person's name. Behind him is a row of heads; inside the heads, brains. I don't know any of the heads, nor do I know the brains. However, all the people who have come are extremely polite and well dressed, as though they have come here together for an important rehearsal. Oh, yes, the rehearsal is really running on a bit, so one man who has slightly less hair than the one next to him yawns, then moves his left arm and carries out the following movements in sequence:

1. speedily extending his arm to the front
2. bending his arm at the elbow salutation-style
3. fixing his eyes on his wrist

On this day, the ancient event that is taking place has something to do with a coffin. As someone fixes his attention on his wrist-watch, a coffin is being carried down the stairs. The thick ropes and the coffin are fashioned, as deftly as you can imagine, into a lift. The texture of the ropes and the texture of the wood complement each other perfectly, and so do their colours. At this point, many people have a cold.

— Goodbye then
I say.

— Goodbye

I say. After saying that I realize I must take a Beauty Candy when I get home. Beauty Candy is the name of one of the flu medicines we always keep at home. And now Mother takes a bunch of fresh flowers wrapped in cellophane and places it on top of the lift. As the flowers get on this special lift they press "B".

It is a fine, sunny day; the sun has been shining brilliantly since early morning. The sun shines on the yellow and white stripes of a toy horse floating in the swimming pool inside the high walls. The sun shines on a soft drink bottle on a pile of rubble facing the pavilion on the Peak. The sun shines on the tail of an aeroplane by the side of a cloud shaped like a lamb. On fine, sunny days, these are the things the sun loves to do. When the flowers travel down on the lift, the sun also shines on the cellophane wrapping around the flowers, and the silver-white ribbon, tied in a bow, shoots out arrows of light which pierce many eyes. After a while, the arrows are used up, the petals have fallen into the shadow, and of course the smiles on the flowers have nowhere to stay.

Mother kneels down and, very, very slowly, picks up a handful of earth beside her feet. Her movement is so slow that it becomes some kind of trend which is picked up by the wind and spread like an infectious disease: on a football field not far away, the referee, the linesmen, the players on both sides, and even the football are all affected; the game turns into a slow-motion demonstration. Later, there is this river which stops flowing. A crow hangs suspended in the air, turning into some strange weight until "plop —", it falls onto Mother's head.

Mother opens her hand; the earth gradually falls.

— It's raining

— It's snowing

It is probably the ants or the caterpillars that are calling. But Mother will not hear them. All of a sudden she is dedicated to becoming a first-rate gardener, trying her best to grow some sort of mysterious flower. So everyone gives her a hand, gathering handfuls of earth to bury the seeds.

Those who are in work uniforms break open several bags and hold them upside down, also to help with the flower planting. They spread the quick lime as if it's a fertilizer, and soon there is a spotless white screen. All the feet walk through this screen and down the stairs.

— That's it then, goodbye

I say. After saying that I decide not to have the Beauty Candy when I get home; I'll have a Delicious instead. Delicious is also a flu medicine we keep at home, and it's more effective than Beauty Candy.

On Braids' pony tail there is a fluffy white flower[3] with many tiny petals. Yes, it's because of this flower that the lotus roots said,

— You can live there

Mother does not say anything. A breeze rests on the wings of the nameless angel. The staircase standing in front of the white screen stares at her coldly as she looks back with every step.

Sunday morning. On an irregular-shaped lawn a sizable crowd has gathered. This lawn on which so many people are standing is surrounded by black railings. On the railings there are carvings: some sort of time-honoured symbol.

When the sun shines on the railings, it tempts you to climb over and turn a couple of somersaults on the gently sloping lawn. However, no one has actually done it. Those who get the idea either soon drop it, or they go over to the nearby square in front of the bank, watch the water splashing on the colourful tiled wall, finish off an ice lolly, and go home.

The rubbish bins on the square have consumed quite a lot of things today. One of the rubbish bins have consumed this thing:

The centre of the earthquake last night was Badan Village on the Kelakunlun[4] Road thirty-four miles north of Tagete.

There is a very large crowd on the lawn today, but how many people are there exactly? It's tempting to guess. Some say, five thousand; some

---

[3] A white flower made of yarn on a girl's or a woman's head signifies mourning for her close kin, i.e. father, mother or husband.

[4] The Kelakunlun Mountain is in Xinjiang's 新疆 Uighur region.

say, seven thousand; some say, nine thousand two hundred and five. That figure, nine thousand two hundred and five, seems to be a number checked by the authorities and then published. People all think that the government press officer is here.

And then someone shouts loudly: Thirteen thousand. A nearby auction house is auctioning a clay bowl from the Qianlong period of the Qing dynasty. The auctioneer hears the words "thirteen thousand", repeats it three times, and as no one comes up with a higher bid, he deals a heavy blow with his hammer. It's unusual for an antiques auction to be held here on a Sunday.

In this place Sundays are holidays. The citizens are either still in bed, or they have gone to places for swimming, places for hiking, places for fishing, places for sight-seeing and people-watching, places for early morning dim-sum, places for queuing for tickets for the early morning show, or they are having their dim-sum, or they are fishing.

Some people don't like fishing; they like taking along an extra eye when they go out. When they cross the street, one eye looks right, another eye looks left, yet another eye looks right again. Walk slowly; walk and cross along the road.[5]

One fellow who has brought an extra eye along has a travel bag on his shoulders big enough to hold two geese. The bag is zipped up. It looks so heavy that you'd think there really are two geese in it. On the travel bag there is a picture of an aeroplane flying around the globe. Just imagine, an aeroplane that will never find an airport to land in, and a world so congested that there's no room for a runway.

Though the man with the bag has an extra eye, he is gripping tightly in both hands some round and long, and some short, photographic instruments. When he walks past the lawn, the grass thinks that a hunter has come.

––––––––––––––

[5] These phrases are taken from government advertisements for road safety, some of which were poorly written in Chinese.

— Cover up the woodpecker, quick

— Cover up the long-eared hare, quick

the grass says. In fact the man with an extra eye has decided to take pictures in Big Trees Garden above, where the cockscombs are in bloom. At the thought of the blooming faces of the flowers, he hurries on in big strides, as though he is afraid that a minute's lingering would cause all those faces in bloom to be snapped up by other lenses. Behind him walk two people carrying a mirror. As they cross the lawn and see that the mirror is filled with faces, they slow down.

— Oh, so many people are looking into our mirror

they say, and so they stop walking and let all those faces take a good hard look, after which they carry the mirror out of sight and into a curtain-walled building.

The receptionist at the information desk of the curtain-walled building is reading a newspaper. No one knows which item of the news he is reading, for behind his chair is a wall unable to divulge his secrets. The mirror which has just arrived has yet to be hung up. However, if one stands in front of the receptionist, at a distance close enough to hear him clear his throat, one would be able to read the editorial on the other side of the paper, which contains the following lines:

Nowadays rice is packed in plastic sacks in many places. As a result the demand for jute is constantly shrinking. Hemp export alone will not be able to support a population of 1,400 per square mile.

With the exception of the many, many faces on the grassy slope, today is no different from any other day — cars still come down from Big Trees Garden along the government drive, pass the Hill-climbing-car Station[6] towards the roundabout, where they go round the mulberry bush,

---

[6] These three places are the Botanical Gardens, Lower Albert Road and the Peak Tram station in Hong Kong's Central District.

the mulberry bush, the mulberry bush, where they go round the mulberry bush, even at five o'clock in the morning. A group of foreigners stand on the balcony of the hotel facing the roundabout,[7] admiring the Orient that stretches out before their eyes.

A little further up is the Stars and Stripes Public Relations Institute.[8] As this is a Sunday — Sabbath day — its doors are closed. Outside the building a cleaning team and a water-spraying vehicle are working together to clean up the road. As the water-spraying vehicle splashes water and rotates the two huge round brushes protruding from under both sides of its belly, a pile of wastepaper has been swept together, waiting to be taken onto the garbage truck.

At this moment, a man who walks like a pair of rusty scissors comes up to the pile of garbage and picks up from amongst the wastepaper a large, torn piece of old newspaper. The members of the cleaning team can see what he is doing, of course, but no one would begrudge him the pleasure of reading a sheet of old newspaper which contains just the following news item:

Israel will not give up strategic Metulla and Ein Gedi, or the Abu

Rudeis oil fields in Sinai

The man who has picked up these printed words, immediately upon grabbing hold of the sheet of paper, lifts one leg in dancing-stork posture and presses the paper hard against the sole of his shoe. It takes him quite a bit of effort to get rid of a piece of stuck-fast chewing gum. After that he throws the gum and the old newspaper back onto the pile of garbage, and then walks away smartly. As a result the chewing gum sticks to the Abu Rudeis oil fields.

At this moment, quite a large crowd has gathered outside the railings of the sloping lawn. It is like a race: the pistol is fired, and the race begins. Result: the number of people is greater inside the railings; the noise is greater outside.

---

[7] The Hilton Hotel.
[8] The U.S. Consulate.

— Ooh, they've come to petition

The man who is in exclamation mode thought that all these people gathered on the lawn had come to apply for helicopter licences.

— Who is it that said we're protesting against Sunday rain

The man who says this is carrying a huge black umbrella under his arm. Just as everybody is about to engage in some pleasantries, their attention is handed over to a newcomer on a motorcycle. The newcomer is wearing a yachting outfit, a crash helmet and spiked running shoes. He leaves his motorcycle at the roadside, instructing it to lie down, then he pushes through the crowd and squeezes himself through to the front, where his nose almost breaks one of the iron railings. He thrusts his hands sideways, his thumbs landing on the ears of his fat pants; the two ears were originally meant to help balance a belt. Now that his hands are hanging so heavily on them, his pants almost come off.

— Is it a BBQ

— Is it a BBQ

He asks repeatedly. This is a man who likes fun and excitement. Seeing that there is only sunlight on the lawn, no fire, he is deeply disappointed.

Another man who has come by motorcycle is a reporter. He has come with a friend. After they get here, his friend takes his helmet from him, ties it to the back of the motorbike, steps on the kickstarter and putt-putts off. At this moment, the man whose thumbs are hanging on the ears of his fat pants catches sight of the departing motorcycle. He hurriedly pushes his way through the crowd, gets back to where he has left his motorbike, starts the engine, and follows the trail of the other bike. Everyone can hear him shouting:

— Hey, I'll race you

— Hey, I'll race you

Very soon, he is out of sight. Everyone knows that the man who has just got here is a reporter; there's a reporter's identification tag pinned to his shirt, showing his very own photograph in full colour. He walks a few paces and then starts running. In no time he comes to the lawn.

— Is there no other solution

He is talking into a loudspeaker which looks like a spray can, asking people on the lawn for their opinions.

At this moment, at the side of the square not very far from the lawn, a ferry boat has just left the pier. A man sitting on the upper deck beside a row of lifebuoys starts humming along as soon as he hears the Harbour Big Ben launch into its tradition-honoured tune, and as the clock strikes he follows suit, counting to ten. He has no idea that there is a crowd gathered on the lawn; in fact he has no idea that there is such a lawn in the city. He is just sitting on the ferry boat, looking casually at the oarless junks, and at the sea which contains so many things and yet shows you nothing on the surface. There is a package at the man's side. He had put it on the seat next to him right after he boarded. It is a pack of salted fish wrapped in an out-of-date newspaper. The paper is worn and fuzzy, there are even oil stains on it, but the words printed there can still be made out. They read:

A bright blue object, surrounded by three belts of light, was intermittently visible in the sky over the eastern coast of Australia for three hours.

As there is absolutely nothing for him to do on the ferry boat, and it is such a very fine day with such a soothing sea breeze, the owner of the salted fish soon falls asleep.

2

Sunday afternoon. Some people say: Sunday, nothing much to do. Let's play mahjongg. The four of them are just the right number for the game, so they bring out a folded table, unfold it, and pour out a whole tableful of translucent jelly candies.

When four people sit down at the mahjongg table, the atmosphere is full of excitement. They all hit their mahjongg tiles hard against the table, as though whoever makes the loudest noise is going to win, or even if he doesn't win, his posture makes him look like a winner. Four people seated at the mahjongg table are fond of talking in a loud voice as they shuffle the tiles; they all talk about what happened during the previous set or game.

Besides making a loud noise with the mahjongg tiles and talking in a loud voice, they also like to turn on the TV to fuel their excitement (the fact that they turn on the TV is of course not the TV's fault). Entertainment offered by the seven TV channels plus the ads is enough fuel for all they want to talk about. So, in this 300-square-foot squarish flat that is sitting- and bed- room all in one, the atmosphere couldn't be more excited.

The flat where these four are playing mahjongg is very small. Though it is *called* a flat, in fact it's just a 300-square-foot room (the fact that it's a 300-square-foot room is of course not the 300-square-feet's fault). The room includes a kitchen where even the fridge has nowhere to stand, and a bathroom where a pair of wooden sandals finds it hard to move around. As for the bath-tub, you

don't see it when you walk in because it is placed inside the picture hanging at the back of the door (the fact that it is on the picture at the back of the door is of course not the door's fault).

A 300-square-foot room can, of course, be divided into several even smaller rooms. On the iron gate at the main entrance downstairs, there is a red piece of paper with the following words clearly written on it: Middle room[1] for rent. People who have seen this piece of paper have also had a look at the room. They say: so, it's actually a wall unit of a brand new design, with simplicity of line as its outstanding characteristic. They suggest to the owner of the flat that this wall unit should be dispatched to the Mediterranean Cultural Association so that it can take part in next autumn's furniture fair.

The owners of the flat where four people are playing mahjongg have not divided up their flat. They have only placed three heavy, clumsy wooden beds at right angles to each other, all pushed against the walls (the fact that they have only placed three heavy, clumsy wooden beds at right angles to each other pushed against the wall is of course not the beds' fault). Two of the beds are actually bunk beds. Besides the beds the following have also been squeezed in: two wardrobes, a dining table and its six chair-friends, two camphor-wood chests and two chests of drawers shouldering a TV set between them. The colourful items in the flat are the chests of drawers.

Though available space is limited, it does not cause much of a problem for the mahjongg players. They have still managed to unfold the folding table beside the door, and a fair number of TV programmes have come and gone. However, playing mahjongg in this flat does have its problems. First, in hot weather there is no air-conditioning, just an electric fan which always blows their hair into a mess and sometimes blows their minds into a mess. Second, whenever someone rings the doorbell, the game of mahjongg must stop, and two of the four players must endure

---

[1] When there are three rooms in a row, the one in the middle is usually the darkest, most poorly ventilated and therefore least desirable.

the punishment of going to stand in the kitchen (the fact that two players must stand in the kitchen is of course not the kitchen's fault) so that the door can be opened. They have just given a demonstration of this not long ago because Liberty, wearing a pair of grey sandals, has just come back.

A while ago, Liberty was wearing a pair of white sandals, sunbathing as she walked down the main road. The place where she was sunbathing is right outside Harbour Building, a spot called Fat Sha Tsui.[2] There are always people coming and going, some sunbathe, some watch the sea, or they watch the ships. The sailors on the ships sometimes put on a performance of long-distance-cleaning the anchors of sand and mud using a very long hose. Sometimes the ships are surrounded by small junks which are busy giving them a face-wash. All this, you don't get to see from your own window.

The Harbour Building where Liberty went for a walk is a building of winter-warmth and summer-cool, shaped like a runway on the ocean. It is surrounded by water on three sides, where ships are berthed, and linked to the land on one side, where it extends into a corridor along which shops bloom. The lobby on the ground floor is fond of flower arrangement shows, exhibitions of tables and chairs that quarrel with the classical, and cars. On rare occasions, there are even Come-one-come-all concerts. That is why the place is packed full every Sunday.

Today, there is an art exhibition in the lobby of the Harbour Building. As soon as Liberty walked in, she met an oil drum whose body had been painted all white. It was standing on the wood parquet floor of the lobby, with a few words on its side, all written in different colours of paint. The words said: I'm hungry (the fact that the oil drum is hungry is of course not the oil drum's fault).

By the side of the oil drum there was a water tap which had been turned on — you saw a chain of round or not-so-round circles coming out

---

[2] This refers to the area outside the Ocean Terminal in Tsim Sha Tsui. Because of land reclamation, the word Tsim, or pointed, is no longer an accurate description.

of it. This water tap was framed in a picture with a floating white bubble, the kind of bubble used for dialogue in a comic strip. The bubble in the picture floated next to the mouth of the water tap. Written inside: I'm thirsty (the fact that the water tap is thirsty is of course not the tap's fault).

On the floor in front of the oil drum was lots of grass, but the grass was black (the fact that the grass was black was of course not the grass' fault), as black as burnt toast. At one corner on the grass there was a rectangular plaque which normally read: Keep off the Grass, but now read: Make Me Green Again.

At one end of the patch of grass was a flight of stairs that lead to the first floor. A child was sitting underneath the staircase, holding a notebook in his hands. The notebook was open at page one, revealing its printed contents.

The child was not a part of the art exhibition. He had come to sell raffle tickets for the society for the protection of children. As Liberty walked past him,

— Please buy a raffle ticket

he said. He was obviously tired, that was why he sat underneath the staircase in the lobby.

Today, at the entrance to Harbour Building, a few tousled-haired smiling youths disinclined to shut their smiling mouths were handing out pieces of paper for everyone to read. Some people, averse to making friends with pieces of paper depicting angels, walked in a zig-zag to avoid them. But one person pre-empted the youths, saying he knew it all: For on this day in the city of David a saviour was born, and it was Christ the Lord. You will see a baby wrapped in cloth lying in a stable, and that will be the sign.

Some people didn't have the time to read it, so they stuffed it into their pockets, and, after a while, into a garbage bin. Liberty did not stuff the piece of paper into a garbage bin, she read it. This is what she read:

Sun white sun
White sun white

If I wake up to see a fine day, I am glad
If I wake up to see a fine day and the cows eating grass and you
    drinking milk, I am glad
If I wake up to see a fine day and the cows eating grass and you
    drinking milk and we all sit down to recite a poem, I am glad
If I wake up to see a fine day and the cows eating grass and you
    drinking milk and we all sit down to recite a poem which says
    there is a couple with nineteen kids riding on a smiling hippo,
    I am glad
Glad I am glad
I am glad I am

When Liberty comes home she brings back a box of crayons and two
cartridge paper sketch books.

— How are you

Liberty says. Everyone says some you're fine I'm fine and then
settles down to whatever they want to do. Liberty wants to draw. She sits
down at the dining table, opens a sketch book and takes her crayons out.
She draws a tall fellow with curly hair, a shorty with two splotches of
rouge on her cheeks, and nineteen kids wearing pony tails and braids and
long straight hair and curly hair, all riding on a smiling hippo. Liberty
cannot remember whether a hippo has four toes or five toes, and so she
goes over to the trunk by the wooden bed to search for a picture book of
animals. Liberty has a trunk.

Liberty's trunk was originally an apple crate. It's packed full. The
picture book that Liberty is looking for is somewhere near the bottom.
Every time she needs to take it out, she has to take out some of the things
lying on top of it. And then she has to put them back.

The things Liberty has taken out are: a piece of paper from a candy
box, the kind you meet as soon as you open a box of candy; a piece of
uneven foam rubber originally meant for the protection of Liberty-knows-
not-what; a wooden fish which is actually just a piece of wood cut into
the shape of a fish; a high-stem-glass with a chip at the mouth; a wine
bottle she has picked up in the street, wearing its hoola skirt.

There is this person whose view of everything in the world is as follows:

Things which make good displays, e.g. orchids, sculptures: 5 points

Things which satisfy your appetite, e.g. steaks, snails: 30 points

Things which you wear to show off, e.g. fur coats, diamonds: 30 points

Things which bring you a big reputation, e.g. masterpieces of art and literature: 100 points

Things which can be traded for a mention on the Queen's lists, e.g. charity, high official posts: 1000 points

Things which can be sold in the future for an astronomical price, e.g. real estate, securities: 3000 points

The things in Liberty's apple crate are worth 0 points. That is why Liberty's apple crate is in fact a garbage bin. Liberty has found her picture book. Unfortunately the hippo is standing in the river, so its toes cannot be seen. Liberty decides to please herself. She draws a hippo with four toes.

At this moment, the mahjongg players all stand up beside the river of translucent jelly candies. They take over each other's seats and start playing again.

— Are we disturbing you

saying this, the mahjongg players turn down their volume a little.

— No, I must be boring you

says Liberty. She picks up the two cotton blouses she left on the bed this morning, and walks into the kitchen. Liberty does not have a washing machine. She bought a raffle ticket at Harbour Building just now, but even if they were to deliver a washing machine here, there would be no space for it.

In fact Liberty likes to hand wash her clothes. She is not fond of machines. A lift is a machine that saves you the climbing motion of your legs, but it is also an invention that traps people in a tiny room during power cuts. The push-button on a bus is a machine that controls the doors and the fares, but it is also an invention that makes two ticket collectors and one door guard redundant.

Liberty pours some washing powder into a plastic basin, then places the basin under the water tap so that the powder is dissolved by the force of running water. The washing powder churns up a thin layer of white suds, then settles down into non-reaction. Liberty reads the instructions on the box, which reminds her that it's low-suds washing powder, a new product made for washing machines.

Last week, two door-to-door salesgirls rang the doorbell, both of them stutterers. Their faces were porcelain pale; their eyes, dispirited; their bags, heavy. When you buy washing powder under such circumstances it is only natural that you don't pay attention to the brand.

Low-suds soapy water doesn't even afford you the fantasy of blowing bubbles. Liberty washes her clothes in the sudsless water, which feels strange. It's like swallowing a vitamin C tablet while telling yourself that it's the same as eating a sun-and-water-filled orange. The feeling of swallowing a vitamin C tablet is not the same as eating a juicy orange (the fact that swallowing a vitamin C tablet is not the same as eating a juicy orange is of course not the tablet's fault).

Liberty soaks the blouses for a short while and then quickly rinses them. She hangs them next to the solitary window in the kitchen, on the wooden rail which has been nailed there for the specific purpose of hanging dripping laundry. When dusk comes and it is time to turn on the gas stove, Liberty must take her clothes down and hang them in the bathroom. Wet clothes are such a problem when they drip.

The mahjongg players decide not to cook any dinner; cooking dinner on a Sunday is just a drag. They unanimously decide that in a while they will make some instant noodles called Three Minutes. After arriving at their decision, they continue their game of mahjongg with unrelenting courage.

Liberty is standing in the kitchen, standing in front of the window, standing in what little space is left by the dripping laundry (the fact that she stands in what little space is left by the dripping laundry is of course not the laundry's fault). She can see the tin roofs on the buildings below the window glittering with a burning heat. On one of the tin sheets there is a whole roof-ful of satsuma peel, every one of them turned inside out, revealing their white bellies. Seen from afar, they look like so many cauliflowers. A tree that grows from a crack in the wall seems to have dust lying all over its leaves (the fact that dust seems to lie all over the leaves is of course not the dust's fault). Sometimes cats come up to the roofs to stretch themselves, but not just now. There are only the funny-shaped hair combs standing neatly in a row, all pointing their huge teeth in the same direction. Perhaps from now on young migratory birds will be able to come south on their own.

Had it been night time Liberty would have seen the buildings which are further away shining forth in bluish green and reddish yellow. The reddish yellow may very well be light bulbs, the bluish green fluorescent tubes. Some windows would be uncoloured; perhaps they use moonlight.

At night, or on days of colourless skies, there would be a red light hanging in the air behind the buildings, flashing its signals at the same rate as a normal heartbeat. It tells the aeroplanes flying above:

— I am a mountain

What the aeroplanes give it in return is sky-shattering noise (the fact that aeroplanes give it nothing but sky-shattering noise is of course not the aeroplanes' fault).

   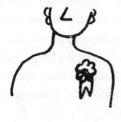

3

They have brought along ten bamboo baskets, each the size of four dustbins. They have also brought along a few bundles of tape and a pile of old canvas in indistinct colours and embarrassing shapes. They have also brought along their hands and shoulders, their feet and all of their voluntary muscles.

They have come to help us move house. I said, move it. I thought they were going to put their arms round the house and move it to wherever we're going. But they shook their heads. What *is* moving house? Of course I have to ask. Come exercise with us, they say. I do as they say, and sure enough I learn what moving house means.

Moving house is: wrap all bowls, plates, cups and spoons individually in tissue paper or old newspaper, turning them into unidentifiable, mysterious, nameless objects, then put them into a plastic bucket. The bucket should be lined with towels, or maybe socks. The bucket was originally meant to store drinking and cooking water during grade-three water-rationing,[1] but during non-rationing seasons it can

---

[1] In the late 1960s and early 1970s Hong Kong experienced severe water shortage, which resulted in water-rationing. Grade-three rationing meant four hours of water supply every day. The worst case happened at the end of the 1960s, when there were four hours of water supply every four days. The problem was largely solved when Hong Kong started purchasing water from southern China, but as recently as 1992 the government still warned of the potential need for water rationing due to a shortage in annual rainfall, on which Hong Kong's water supply is heavily dependent.

be used to store rice, or used as a rubbish bin, according to the owner's pleasure.

Moving house is: take some of the overcoats and all of the two-kilo-each jeans out of the wardrobe, stuff them into the belly of a bed sheet, and tie a knot on top. Mine is a reef knot. As for the pillows, blankets and quilts on the bed, they are rolled up into the thickness of a buffalo and tied up tightly with tape.

From the kitchen, pans, spatula, chopsticks, water jugs, noodles, biscuits, vermicelli, mushrooms, ginger, dates, rock sugar, garlic, bean paste sheets, packets of vegetable soup are all taken out and piled into the bamboo baskets they have brought along. In also go the towels, tooth brushes, tooth paste, shampoo, round mirror, hair dryer, as well as thermometer, gentian violet, iodine, and sterilized bandages.

And, the ugliest, strangest, most trivial, most useless-but-a-pity-to-throw-away, and most forgotten things have all been dug out and put into their bamboo baskets. These include shoe-boxes. Go–sh, twenty-six of them! And we only have two pairs of shoes each.

Moving house is: sweeping out seven bins of garbage and three drawers of dust. The dust has of course rolled into balls, and inside these balls are a dozen or so blunted toothpicks, a few cockroaches lying on their back, a clothes peg, several five-cent coins, a very short pencil with its rubber head intact. There is also a small tin of Tiger Balm, all dried up, looking like a map marking provincial boundaries.

Moving house is terminating the lifespan of many things in the process of a revolution. These things include two clay cooking pots which are slightly cracked, in fact one is not cracked but the lid is missing; a pile of old *Life* magazines, a pair of slippers burst at the seams, a paint brush, a calendar, an old mop, six kilos of newspapers, a bundle of no-longer-respectable-looking clothes, and two oil cans.

Moving house is also: watching an acrobatic show. Two gorilla-arms move away a wardrobe; one tiger-strength back bears away a fridge. One man takes away eight chairs in one go, and then comes back for two cylinders of gas and an ironing board. They shake their heads at my records, saying the bowl-dance[2] is not on their programme.

So *that* is moving house.

The above is Part 1.

Intermission: Five Minutes. Let's go out for a soft drink.

Moving house is a very fat novel. Part 2 is all about taking everything out of the bamboo baskets they have brought along, e.g. dusters, bleach, washing powder, rose water with a maxi-dress trademark, a paraffin stove with newly trimmed wick, antiseptic, matches with hotel names printed on the box, clothes-hangers, glasses sporting a pattern of dots, and a shopping basket put in its temporary resting place.

Sweaters go into a drawer, scissors go into the sewing box. Shoe-boxes are pushed under the bed, the rice-cooker is put on the kitchen worktop. Beauty Candy and Delicious go into the red-cross-mirror box. An iron, with nowhere to go, is put back on the floor. *Thumbs-up Weekly*[3] also lies on the floor.

Moving house is: an incident during which one of the wardrobes will definitely get a bad scratch on its face. It is also an incident during which you look for a bottle of ink or a stamp and find that you are lost. It is also an incident after which you wake up the next morning to find that you don't know your own front door. However, moving house is good for slimming. I lost a kilo in weight, our house lost 600 kilos.

At the end of it, they take their ten bamboo baskets, and their bundles of tape, and their canvas in embarrassing shapes, and their two buckets of sweat, and their total receipts from the acrobatic show, and leave.

After they have gone, one of my feet says to me: Look, over there, there's a comfortable couch. I look sideways. There are three couches in front of me, one shaped like a winter melon, the other two like sweet

---

[2] A popular acrobatic dance in which the dancers balance piles of bowls on their heads and hands.

[3] 大姆指, a successful literary weekly aimed at secondary and post-secondary students, was published in the mid-1960s and folded in the mid-1970s. It nurtured a whole generation of Hong Kong writers, including Xi Xi.

potatoes. All three are covered in pale yellow upholstery fabric on which the gold-threaded patterns have disappeared, but which gives out a smell of dryness baked in the sun. In a corner between two couches stands a tall lamp. On the lamp shade is a low-ranking official, with his wife standing at his side, and her daughter standing at her side, and her maid standing at the daughter's side, and a parrot standing at the maid's side, and a low-ranking official standing at its side, and again his wife standing at his side, and again her daughter ....

And again her maid. The picture looks very pale. Diagonally from the sofas, there is an upright piano that is in need of a good dose of calcium. Half of its keys refuse to stand up after they are pressed down. This proves one thing: piano keys and basketballs are things with very different temperaments.

Next to the piano is a TV set. It is brand new, a house-warming present from the water-lilies. It was delivered a week ago, and all the channels have been fine-tuned.

I install myself speedily on a couch, and I'm not going to get up again. After sitting down, I strike up an acquaintance with the TV set and come across a TV series. It's called Super-Supermarket. It's called that because the supermarket featured in it is slightly larger than the others inhabiting the same small town, that's all.

The director of this series is very fond of introducing the audience slowly and lovingly to various supermarket scenes, hoping that the audience will appreciate the different levels of meaning of these scenes as they would a masterpiece of art. The drawback of this approach is: you feel that the pace is not fast enough.

This supermarket is housed in a 100-storey building. Its total area is equal to thirty-one Olympic-size football fields. Admittedly it is fairly well-stocked. People can buy most of their daily necessities here, and if they want a school or a village, they can place an advance order. Anyone looking for anything will probably find it in this supermarket: minibanks, restaurants, cafés, swimming pool, cinema, park, train, sunshine, friends, moon, etc. The supermarket prints a sumptuous yellow-pages catalogue every year, a copy of which is sent to the town library. As for the rest, because no one can move them, and even if they could, no front door is big enough for them to get through, they are all dumped into the landfill.

This evening, the supermarket series tells the story of a man called Big Feet. The only thing that distinguishes Big Feet from other people is that his feet are a little bigger than normal. Big Feet's mother is a woman given to chortling who weighs ninety kilos. This day, while she is at the supermarket looking for glutinous rice flour, her insides bite into her real hard and render her immobile. The staff at the Super-supermarket take her to the hospital on the nineteenth floor straight away, and there Big Feet is born.

The chairperson of the Super-supermarket's board of directors (i.e. the wife of the vice-chairperson of the board of directors) and the vice-chairperson of the board (i.e. the husband of the chairperson), together with the president, the vice-president, the general manager and the deputy general manager hold an emergency meeting to deal with this exciting event. It is agreed that the board will award Big Feet's mother a huge cash prize and Big Feet a book of free coupons good for one century, which means that whatever Big Feet needs to buy from the supermarket, he can have for free. What is more, everyone decides that they should keep Big Feet there, in the care of a private nurse. Big Feet's mother need not worry about his future education funds either.

The Super-supermarket is doing all this because after several hundred years of birth control, the local population has dwindled to the point where there aren't enough people to eat all the beetroot in the fields. The beetroot is thrown into the river, where there are so many fish that they get squeezed up onto the shore. That is why the family that has a baby not only earns itself a large grant from the government, it also brings great joy to the whole town.

And so Big Feet's mother leaves Big Feet in the Super-supermarket and goes on a grand tour of Mars the very next day. After Big Feet has grown a bit, he becomes very fond of the Super-supermarket. He refuses to go home when his mother comes to pick him up, and so she goes on a grand tour of Neptune.

Big Feet spends his carefree days in the Super-supermarket, watching TV day and night on the sixty-ninth floor. He picks up all sorts of knowledge from the TV. By the age of seventeen he has finished the whole curriculum offered by the Future Dept. of the Highest Education Institute; he has also mastered the Universal Language and the Akuaku tongue.

Beds are sold on the twenty-fifth floor. Customers are welcome to try them out, and those who sleep the soundest can win a grand prize: Galaxy silver coins and 99% of the votes for the next visiting membership on the town council. When Big Feet is tired of watching TV he goes to sleep in these beds; his big feet stretched out on the eiderdown at the end of the bed are most eye-catching. His posture is serene and peaceful. And so Big Feet wins the grand prize. They open a drawing account in the bank for him, and stuff a long pad into his pocket. Every time he draws a flower, he can exchange it for beautiful Galaxy silver coins. Big Feet fills the book with flowers and then gives it to a little girl playing hide-and-seek.

One day, for some unknown reason, Big Feet does not wake up despite having slept for three whole days. By now, because he has won the grand prize, he is already a councillor. However, he knows nothing about it. And by now, Big Feet's mother is on a grand tour of the sun. She sends back a photo of herself in the company of a black hole, but Big Feet does not get to see it. According to the doctor's report, Big Feet has no interest in waking up. And so everyone sends him more presents, mostly flowers. Those on the ninety-eighth floor send a marble statue of Angel Big Feet.

The Super-supermarket comes last in the town's TV ratings. So starting from next week, a different programme will be aired this time slot, a traditional family-oriented romantic musical series, called The Woman Warrior.

4

There is this envelope with my name written on it. It's a long, well-fed, potato-skin coloured envelope stuffed with thick folded paper. Were this envelope to be sent overseas, you'd need to add quite a few high denomination stamps to it, thus greatly increasing the postage. That is something you cannot afford not to know.

My name, i.e. Fruits, is written on the envelope, so is my address, i.e. Rear Unit, Block B, 11/Fl (12th Chinese-level), Carrots Building, 199 Cabbage St, Little Woods. You can see why the postman doesn't have it easy. In fact the address on the envelope is no longer my address. Now I live in No. 1 Hobby Horse Road. An address like that gladdens me every time I write to my friends because it saves me a lot of ink, and it's difficult to get it wrong.

The words on the envelope are not handwritten; it's the lettering of a machine. This machine's registered title is typewriter. It is smaller than a piano, makes a more monotonous noise than a piano, takes less time to learn to play than a piano, has less artistic value than a piano, and is therefore cheaper than a piano. This is called direct proportion. That is something you cannot afford not to know.

Experts who research into the problems of human environmentalism have pinpointed the problem with this machine's lettering, saying that it carries the coldness of industrial civilization. This is a feeling quite different from that which comes with

a good cold drink on a hot day. That is something you cannot afford not
to know.

Originally there was no reason for anyone to send me such a letter;
they didn't know me, and I didn't know them. But a few weeks ago they
printed a notice in the newspapers informing us of one thing. The original
was more detailed, of course, but the gist was:

We are the Telephone Company

We are recruiting technicians

We will provide the necessary training

I had just finished my School Certificate Exam and was looking for
something interesting to do so that I could take myself to lunch every day
and also take my sister Braids to lunch. I decided that I should do
something interesting; no coldness of the industrial civilization for me.

I saw "We are the Telephone Company", "We are the Library", "We
are the Swimming Pool". I liked "We are the Telephone Company", and
so I said to them:

I am Fruits

I want to be a technician

Train me

They have sent my letter box a brown envelope the colour of dried
satsuma peel, stuffed with leaves of paper inside. On one of the leaves
there are many words; they read like this after my translation:

You said you want to work for us. Point noted. But we don't know
who you are, whether you are tall or short, fat or slim, whether you like
fishing or not, so we have enclosed the other pages in this letter. We are
asking you to play (just a formality) this game of crosswords so that we
will understand each other better. Thank you for your help.

I fill in sections A and B with a fountain pen. What I fill in are: Last
Name. First Name. ID Card No. Date of Birth. Place of Birth. Nationality.
Address. Schools Attended. Grades. From date, month, year to date,
month, year.

At this moment some objects appear on my desk. One of them is my
graduation certificate with a photo of my discomposed countenance, a

recent passport-size photo. I had two dozen prints of this recent photo made, which made me broke for a whole weekend. The eleventh photo I have just stuck on Section C of the form I filled in.

Besides my graduation certificate and my photos, there is also my ID card. Admittedly it is small, but it has great self-defence power. It is humidity proof, corrosion proof, bug proof and no-starching drip-dry.

The section I like best is Section D because it points at itself and says: No need to fill in this section.

I didn't post this form because they said that I could hand it in in person. So that's what I did. They ask us to sit in a classroom. I call it a classroom because there is a blackboard in it. I say us because besides me, there are others like me who want to work for them.

They hand us some sheets of paper and ask us first to do some sums and then to write a composition. There is a passage in English which they ask us to translate into Chinese. And so I translate:

When you pick up the phone, how do you give the other party a good impression? What tone of voice should you adopt?

As I get to this point, I forget that I am translating. I think it may be a questionnaire, and so I answer: The best tone of voice is that of a foreign president delivering a speech. Once, I watched a high-resolution live satellite transmission on TV, I heard a president being sworn in. His voice was beautiful. Too bad I can't remember which president it was, but that's not my fault. What can one do about all these foreign presidents playing musical chairs?

The composition should be in English. The requirement is 100 to 150 words. The topic is "The Future". I have no idea whether they want to know about my future, or our common future, or the future of their small group, so I just write down whatever I feel like, and it reads:

In the future, I hope that I will be able to make phone calls to the moon (10-20), or perhaps further away, to Saturn (20-25), or perhaps even to the Milky Way. I'd like to talk to the extraterrestrials on other planets (30-40).

I have two reasons for writing like this.

First, I received a letter a while ago, not a typed letter, a hand-written one. The letter was sent from a ship; it took thirty-six days to reach me. One of the things it says is: Fruits, how glorious it would be if we could shout at each other over the phone. When my letter-writing friend wrote this letter, he was on a ship, and the ship was in the Pacific Ocean. The Pacific Ocean is of course not very far away, but if you can't talk on the phone while you're there, you might as well be on Saturn.

Second, some people say that the gods we have believed in for thousands of years may, perhaps, possibly, very likely, be astronauts from other planets who came for a visit.

If that is true, why don't we talk (to them) on the phone? Something like, long time no see, how've you been? It's day (time) here, what (time) is it over there? We have 365 (days) a year, how many (days) have you got? And then, we can invite them to come to tea.

I hand in the word-filled piece of paper to the people in front of the blackboard. There are two of them, two smiling mouths. That is the difference between this classroom and other classrooms. All the classrooms I remember only have one person in front of the blackboard, and that one person is against smiling. That person who is against smiling likes to ask questions. The following is one of the questions:

You can trade five apples for three pears
You can trade three pears for two oranges
You can trade two oranges for five mangoes
How many apples will you get for six pears

One voice said: I wonder whether the apples are red or green. Another voice said: What happened to bananas. The following is another question:

There is a water jug
Fill a 1 ½ litre container
and a 2 ¾ litre container
and a 3 ⅝ litre container
all to full capacity
Pour all the water into the jug

and the jug is just full

What is the capacity of the jug

One voice said: Best if it's a jug of ice-cold soft drink. And another voice said: A jug with two ears looks more balanced than a jug with one.

After looking at my sums and composition, the two people in front of the blackboard say that I should also visit the classroom on the other side. I walk over at full speed. Only one person is sitting there in front of the blackboard, but this person also likes to smile. I tell him: I've met three rainbows today.

— And your name is

he says. At this moment, he opens the folder in his hands, a file containing a piece of paper with my recent passport-size photo on it, and my name written next to the photo. I am truly puzzled. But after a while I figure it out. What else could he have said? Could he say, it's such a fine day, let's go swimming?

Or perhaps, have you had breakfast? Would you like a Spanish coffee?

This person who also likes to smile asks me to read aloud a passage in English. I have taken two Beauty Candies today, and so my voice is like a blower, whizzz–whizzz–. Seeing this, he recommends that I have a medical, and gives me a free coupon. I thank him, wishing him good health and good exam results. And since it will soon be Christmas, I also wish him Merry Christmas and Happy New Year. And so we part company. After we part, two things occur to me:

First, there can be more than one person in front of the blackboard, and it is not necessary to not smile.

Second, when people meet for the first time, they should ask each other's names instead of just saying: The weather today is Hahaha.

The place where they invite me to go for a medical is the Horns Medical Centre. The Horns Medical Centre is near the Dilemma Ferry Pier where the shops nearby all have pink telephones. On this day all the people who have come to Horns for their medical have free coupons; I haven't seen anyone without a coupon. As I enter the door I announce that I am Fruits, and so no one asks if he or she may have my name. They only tell me to follow the people in front of me.

The crowd of people standing in front of me seem to be queuing, but they could also just be standing there. Some of them are in white shorts and sneakers, some are wearing sports caps and have taken off their shirts, which they drape over one shoulder. I'm happy to see this, for I'm sure we're going to have a game of football outside later on. But as I walk in, I realize that it is no football field on the other side of the door; it is a toilet. As for me, I am holding no football in my hand, but a bottle.

Since there is no football field, after a very short while I go to stand on the scales and from that I learn I am no elephant. And as a ruler lands on the top of my head, I realize I am no cotton tree. Someone puts a tick-ticking watch at the back of my head; I say it's on the right, and it really is on the right. Someone hits my knees for absolutely no reason at all, and so I tell him I don't like films depicting violence. I also dislike an ashen-faced piece of glass that forbids me to breathe and eats up many first class soldiers in my body.

Someone asks me to open my mouth wide, no doubt taking me for a horse. Someone shows me a picture of boiling water with blue and green bubbles and asks me to find a red bubble hidden there; I find it. I also have a look at an eye-test sheet where letters turn somersaults, you know the kind: Ε ɱ Ǝ ɯ. Someone ties one of my arms up and jabs it with a needle. My arm gets very upset so I give it some cotton wool candy. But the strangest of them all is the one who recites to me. I am sure he comes first in every exam, and if he joins one of those quizzes he's sure to win a return air ticket to the Congo. Here he goes:

Chickenpox, trachoma, diphtheria, cholera, typhus, dysentery, malaria, bronchitis, tuberculosis, whooping cough, scarlet fever, typhoid, jaundice, varix, duodenal ulcer, appendicitis, rheumatism, asthma, sleepwalking, kala-azar, oesteromalacia, tinea.

A number of the itises are lost on my ears. He asks whether I have ever had any of them, and I shake my head. I proceed to show him the scar on my foot from my chickenpox vaccination because to me it's a strange shape, like tree rings, but a chickenpox vaccination doesn't seem to interest him.

I'm interested in the pictures hanging on their walls, though. One of them is a bones man, which means the whole person is just made up of bones; he has no heart at all. Then there is this other picture of a nerves man whose tangle of nerves looks as though it's on fire. It is after seeing these pictures that I thought they may be interested in my chickenpox vaccination scar.

None of the people who take their medical with me at the Horns Medical Centre have talked to me, that is, none except one. I was standing on the scales, he was standing beside me, waiting with his shoes off. The cotton top he had on was designed like a sail. He told me that the one wish his socks had was to own a cheese factory some day.

As I leave the Horns Medical Centre, a member of their staff gives me a card. It turns out to be a strange kind of stamp for after I take it in my hands I immediately turn into a walking parcel, and soon I have sent myself to Snow White Building.

The walls of Snow White Building are the colour of a forest. On the walls are pictures of medieval knights, all armoured and equestrian. One of the generals is on a losing streak — someone pointed out that it was probably in his stars — his opponent in black armour has thrust a spear into his throat. Every time I walk past that wall, I hear him cry: The pain the pain, while the victorious knight says: My gain, my gain. Numerous people have heard this dialogue; they all remember it well. Once, some fellow pointed at the victorious knight and said: One for China. Someone in the crowd responded: China, oh the pain.

I am ten minutes early because I follow the instructions on post vans: Post Early. I am standing outside an office of the Telephone Company, looking at people queuing up to pay their phone bills. So you don't have a cheque book. Neither do I. A queue, and a machine going clack-clack. After paying his phone bill, one man empties his pocket of all its bills —

electricity, water, and rates, and hire purchase sewing machine, and income tax. He counts them, then hurries off into the lift. I spend five minutes watching all this. Another five minutes is spent face to face with the coloured telephones in the display window. They are: red like a fire engine, beige like an ambulance, green like a garbage truck, blue like a police van. Though they're all different colours, you can still get a red fire engine to come to you by dialling a blue phone. Amongst all these vehicles, the colour of the fire engine is definitely the brightest, and its standpoint the most clearly stated — it is against fires.

The telephone on the desk is camel-coloured.

— I am Fruits

And who are you? Perhaps you are from the Engineering Department, sir, perhaps you are from the Development Department, sir? I don't know who you are, and since I have told you I am Fruits, could you please let me know who you are?

— I have a mother, called Grace

— I have a sister, called Braids

And who do you have in your family? The little girl in the picture on this desk, that must be your daughter. I'm sure she likes kites. I have a kite too; it's a pity there isn't anywhere where I can fly it.

— I have just finished school

— I took the School Certificate Exam this year

I suppose you have been through many exams as well. Could geography and history have been your favourite subjects at school, too? Geography is interesting, it tells you how huge our space is. As for history, it tells you that time is without beginning and end. Considering that our space is so huge and that there is no beginning or end to time, isn't it a remarkable coincidence that we should be here together, separated by a mere desk? And yet I do not know who you are, and I do not know whether I should ask you what your name is.

— I was born here, in this city

— No, I have never been anywhere else

And you? You must have come from some other city. Is it exciting, that city of yours? Suppose the two of us had lived in a totem society, the situation would have been very different, wouldn't it? We would probably be very close relatives. I would know that when the sun shines on your nose, you would get up and begin your day's work. I would have seen you making a canoe — first of all you burn the part which you want to hollow out, and then you chip away the charred wood with a stone axe. I would also know that you like fish, and so I would bring some fish to swap for the fruits you pick from the trees. But now we live in the age of gravitation, and things have changed so much. There are people everywhere, and our work is so full of tedious details, it really is difficult to get to know one another.

— I like telephones

— they're a means of communication

Now that there is the telephone, do you still write letters? Machines have made us lazy. When script came into being, men no longer needed their memory; when books came into being, men no longer wanted to think. I suppose men are very much like the universe, expansion makes them different from their former selves. Clusters of stars in the universe expand in all directions, with the result that the size of the cluster is enlarged, but the density is lessened. I have read about it somewhere, probably in the school library. The force of universal repulsion is greater than that of gravitation, and that is what prevents things from coming together; instead they move away from each other. You see, even human beings are the same. Oh, the lyrics of a song suddenly come to mind. It's called *Tout va bien*. I can only sing a couple of lines, it goes like this:

As long as the same old sun shines over our heads

Everything is fine

Yes, it's a fine day today. In a while, you can do what you like, and I can do what I like.

The person sitting across the desk writes a chain of words on a piece of paper and hands it to me.

— Young man, make a good job of it

he says.

— I will

I reply. I thank him and come out. Ah, the same old sun shines over my head, the same sun from the eighteenth, fifteenth, twenty-seventh, thirty-ninth centuries. Starting tomorrow I will be able to take myself to lunch, and I can also take my mother Grace to lunch, and also my sister Braids. I'm so happy. My happiness lasts well into the next day.

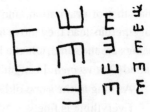

5

Braids has a desk. It is a big wooden desk, with a top large enough for you to skip-rope on. On either side of the desk there are four deep drawers, and right in the middle there is one shallow drawer. Altogether the desk has nine drawers. When Braids first came to No. 1 Hobby Horse Road, the desk was standing alone in the middle of a large room. When Braids saw it, she thought it was a dining table; later she discovered its tentacle-like drawers. So it is now in a room which belongs to Braids. This is a room the desk has never left in the last few decades, a room well hidden from the main road, where strong, healthy guava fruit grow outside the windows. It's very quiet here. As Braids will soon be sitting a school entrance exam, she has chosen this quiet room so that she can study.

Braids has a red hand-operated pencil sharpener which is now fixed to one corner of the desk. Braids comes here to sharpen her pencils about fifty times a day. *Cheep-cheep, cluck-cluck*, that's the sound of Braids sharpening her pencils. The top right hand drawer is filled with presents Braids has received. When her birthday comes, she gets presents. People ask: Braids, what would you like for your birthday? And without stopping to think Braids replies: Pencils. And so she has dozens and dozens of pencils, all HB. Pencils are to Braids what cigarettes are to other people. Some people get through a pack of twenty cigarettes a day; Braids gets

through a pack of a dozen pencils a day.

Braids has a bookcase. It is standing against the wall next to the wooden desk. It's the same height as Braids, but there aren't any books on its shelves. Then *what* is on the shelves, you may very well ask. Well, it's full, packed full with exercise books. There is one shelf of Chinese exercise books, two shelves of Arithmetic ones, and three shelves of English ones. Such is the weight of these exercise books that the bookcase stands half collapsed under it. Braids has therefore christened the poor bookcase The Leaning Tower of Braids. After a while, Braids decides that the overflowing exercise books should just be piled up on the floor. Each exercise book weighs about half a kilo. They're mostly loose-leaf linked together at the two eyes by a shoe-lace type of string which meets in a bow on the cover. The exercises inside are much of a muchness, while the covers are identified by things like 707, 909, 246 or 369. Alternately they read: Best of Chinese Exercises, Categorized English Exercises, or Practical Secondary School Entrance Arithmetic. On all the covers of the arithmetic exercise books is written: Decimal System.

Any normal graduating primary school student leads a life similar to Braids', which means going to school every morning, or every afternoon, or both morning and afternoon. After getting home, aside from having dinner and taking a shower, all their time is spent on homework. Of course they should get to play after homework's finished, but since homework is never finished, they never get to play. Braids goes to school every morning, comes home at one in the afternoon, and by two o'clock sharp she is sitting in front of the window where guava leaves can be seen, her exercise book open, the computer answer sheet waiting to be filled in. She fills in some answers, then sharpens her pencil; fills in some more, then sharpens her pencil again. Braids has a piggy bank that used to be really fat, but now, because she makes piggy give her exercise books all the time, piggy is always complaining of hunger.

Braids has an alarm clock. Except when she is asleep or at school, Braids and her alarm clock are never parted. This alarm clock is tied to a string hanging from Braids' neck. Wherever she goes in the house her alarm clock goes tick-ticking with her. Sometimes Fruits would shout from the rooftop

— There goes the alarm

— You can come and play shuttlecock now[1]

Braids runs up to the rooftop. Since the alarm clock is hanging from her neck, she runs slowly, and she also has to hang onto the alarm clock with one hand. When she plays shuttlecock the alarm clock is left in a corner, but as soon as she finishes, back goes the alarm clock round her neck. Braids' alarm clock sounds every thirty minutes — an interval set by herself. Every time the alarm clock sounds it means Braids has to switch to another task. When the alarm sounds during her game of shuttlecock, she has to go back immediately to her window facing the guava tree and do her homework; when the alarm sounds while she is doing her homework, she has to stop at once and go play shuttlecock or skip, or perhaps draw whatever designs that interest her.

Braids has a schoolbag. Some time after they started growing pot-flowers on the roof, Liberty came with a couple of spring onions, and spring onions proliferated on the rooftop. Some time later, Fruits came back with some chilies, and now there are also chilies on the rooftop. Since there are now so many spring onions on the rooftop, Braids goes there everyday to pick a couple to put into her schoolbag. She says that doing this will help her to know her onions. One day, Fruits asked her: Hey, Clockwork Braids, what if you did know your onions, what'd you do? Braids said that she would create a brave new world.

Braids' desire to create a brave new world shows the influence of her class teacher — a woman who has won the respect and admiration of her whole class. She is a patient teacher, a well-organized person, *and* a kind

---

[1] Chinese children used to make shuttlecocks for this game from old newspapers and cocks' feathers.

one. She has never been known to scold or physically punish a student, yet everyone listens to her, everyone is well-behaved and keeps quiet in her class, there is just no one who doesn't like her. Besides being a good teacher, she is also a caring form mistress, always giving advice to her students, telling them to work hard, to be patient, and to persevere.

Braids remembers her every word. The fact that Braids follows the alarm clock in allocating her time for work and play is of course not the achievement of the alarm clock but that of her class teacher. Once, the class teacher went to a picnic with them, and everyone sat round her on the lawn, chatting. The class teacher said: the world has left much to be desired. We have brought you into this world, but we haven't made it a good enough place for you, we're really ashamed. But there is nothing much we can do, because our power is limited, or perhaps because we are lazy. Whatever it is, except for saying sorry, there is nothing much we can do. We are ashamed, but you don't have to be sad, you don't have to give up. Now that you are here and have seen and learned about this place, you can build a brave new world according to your own ideals, because you are young.

And so Braids has two wishes, wishes which she once wrote down on a notepad immediately after she had put down her exercise book when the alarm clock rang. One of her wishes is the same as Fruit's. The two wishes are:

1. To travel around the world
2. To build a brave new world when I grow up

Braids has a big dictionary which she discovered lying in a desk drawer the day she moved into No. 1 Hobby Horse Road. Now the drawer is occupied by pencils, and the dictionary has fallen out. This big dictionary of Braids' is thicker than the phone book, and it is not kept on the desk. Instead, Braids has put it on her bed and often uses it as a pillow. Occasionally, when she gets dizzy looking at the little squares in the exercise books, she lies down for a while. She lies in bed with her eyes closed, but she doesn't sleep. At such times she likes to pillow her head on the dictionary. It would be nice if the words would put themselves into her head when she puts her head on the dictionary, she says.

Though Braids does not mean to sleep when she puts her head on the dictionary, sometimes she does fall asleep. Even then, the words in the dictionary still refuse to walk into her head. But the exercise books on the desk and on the floor are a different matter. One fine day, they all turned into sandwiches. Some of the covers became bread, and the contents turned into pickles, tomato slices, ham and egg. So many sandwiches! And so Braids had sandwiches in the morning, sandwiches at noon, and sandwiches in the evening. Within three weeks, she consumed all the sandwiches.

Braids has just finished a letter which is now lying on the desk. It reads:

Dear neighbours,

How are you? I am Braids, as in braided hair. Sometimes I am Brains, as in brains trust. On the day I was born my granddad said to me: You're going to make it some day, so I'll call you Brains. That was how I came to be called Brains. After my granddad passed away, my dad said: All I want is for you to be happy; you don't have to worry about making it. You're my daughter, and you must remember the Chinese saying that our body and our hair are our parents' gifts to us, so you must take good care of them, take good care of yourself. I'll change your name to Braids. And so I am also called Braids. As for me, I like Braids better, and so that's the name I choose to use.

My brother Fruits has also given me a name — Clockwork Braids. He said that he had seen some toys which run on clockwork, like clockwork beetles, clockwork ducks, clockwork orange. He said that I behave as though I could be wound up with a key on my back, so he decided to call me Clockwork Braids. Of course I know he said this because I'm inseparable from my alarm clock.

Whatever the case, I am Braids, your next-door neighbour.
You live in No. 3 Hobby Horse Road, and I live in No.1. You
know, that low building with five padlocks on the door and a lot
of low windows; that low building.

It was like this: My mum Grace, my brother Fruits, and me,
Braids, moved into No. 1 Hobby Horse Road a fortnight ago. In
that fortnight I have seen some fairly special things. Since these
things are related to you, I thought, well, yes, I should tell you
about them.

I have to begin with Monday. On Monday my mum said:
Braids, you always look so pale, you should go and get some sun
on the rooftop. And so I went. I decided to kick a shuttlecock for
a while. You know, I have a shuttlecock I made myself.

But when I got to the rooftop I found that it wasn't possible
to play shuttlecock there — there was simply no place to put my
feet, all such places had been taken up by rubbish. And if you
want to know what the rubbish consisted of, here goes: many
many bottle caps, five fruit juice cans, a mountain load of paper
towels, about two kilos of water melon skin, some toy building
blocks — some were chimneys, some rooftops. Also, a coconut
shell, an ear-ring, a tatty quilt, two dolls — one bald, the other
broken-nosed, and two dozen paper aeroplanes. The paper
aeroplanes were all made of sheets from arithmetic exercise
books. There were additions and subtractions on every one of
them, and some bore a few red crosses.

I thought at that time that perhaps our rooftop was an
exposed beach. As the wind came and went, the rubbish was left
there. There must be quite a lot of beaches like that in our city.

Since the rooftop was filled with rubbish, there was no way
I could play shuttlecock. As I stared at the heaps of rubbish, I
saw a squad of ants marching towards a wall. It was *your* wall,
No. 3 Hobby Horse Road, and on that wall were *your* windows,
No. 3. I thought if the ants were to get into your house, that would

mean a lot of trouble for you, so I got hold of a hose, took aim at the ants and flushed them away. My arms hurt from the effort before the ants were finally gone.

Some time after that my brother Fruits came home, and the two of us formed a clean-up conglomerate. We swept and we washed, and it was all dark before we were done. Our rubbish bin was too small for all that rubbish, and we had to use a few cardboard boxes besides. That night, when the rubbish collection man came with his truck, he asked: Have you just hosted a 100-person buffet?

Excuse me a minute, my alarm clock has started ringing.

Then came Tuesday, let's continue.

Tuesday was yesterday. I said to myself: Why don't you go and play skip on the rooftop? And so I went up, only to find that there was no place for me to skip because the place was again filled with rubbish. The paper aeroplanes this time round were not made from arithmetic exercise books, they were from calligraphy exercise books. On one of the aeroplanes was written: Pairs and pairs of socks / Are hanging at our window. On another one was written: Oh wind Oh wind / You I have seen / You lifted up / A squad of kites / A family of hawks / Are blown up to the clouds.

Amongst the rubbish were a one-wheeled bicycle, a bottom-less basket, a little blackboard, two ducks' heads, one fly-catcher, one can of hair spray, one doghouse, one bag of fish-tails, one broken badminton racket, one sprouting ginger, and one huge cactus. My brother Fruits said: I bet the whole of Mexico has been blown here by the wind.

It was then that I saw all the roaches running towards the wall. I tried the hose on them again, but they all started flying around, and I got scared, so I ran away. After a long while, I went back to see what was happening. All I saw was my brother Fruits sweeping up; all the roaches were gone. And so I also started sweeping. We kept at it for a long time, and after we had finished sweeping we gave the floor a good wash, until it got dark again. When the rubbish collection man came with his truck this time, he asked: How many of you are there in this house? I answered: Only four.

And now I have to tell you about today. Early this morning I went to school. I go to school in the mornings, not in the afternoons. After I finished school I came home along Hobby Horse Road. I saw many walls along the road. Most of them were ordinary-looking, with rows of windows on them, like a big cupboard with many drawers. There were two walls which were rather special: there were ads on them. On the first wall was an ad for cigarettes. It was the picture of a lighted cigarette, with smoke coming from it. As the ad was drawn underneath a window, the smoke rose up all the way to the window. I thought: People inside that window are probably coughing all day long because of all that smoke. On the other wall was an ad for cooking oil. There was a frying pan right underneath a window, and the pan was placed on a stove. Smoke was also coming out of the pan. And so I thought: People inside that window are probably all well-done by now.

And as I was looking at all this I thought: Wouldn't it be nice to plant some flowers on the rooftop. That way there will be red and pink morning glories on the wall. People who walk along Hobby Horse Road will then say: Oh, what a pretty wall! What do you think? I told my brother Fruits about this when I got home, and I also telephoned my aunt Liberty.

There goes my alarm clock again. Excuse me.

Now let's continue.

We went up to the rooftop together to plant the flowers. There were actually quite a number of flowerpots on the rooftop, but there was only soil in them, no flowers. We had gone and bought some seeds, some planting soil, and some books on planting flowers. But when we got to the rooftop we became very sad. The rooftop had turned into a rubbish dump again. Corn cobs were all over the place, together with a broken straw hat, a broken gong, a broken ironing board, ice-cream wrappers, a birdless bird cage, and a broken venetian blind. All this broken stuff gave off a rotting smell. And then there were oil-stained workmen's gloves, a torn straw mat, and petal-less flowers. That was just the floor. The walls were covered with bugs of all sorts, red and green, some had shells, others were hairy, some had no legs, others were all legs. The bugs huddled together, as though they wanted to hide the wall from view. We had to invite the rubbish collection man to come up, and he in turn invited his friends. The bugs finally disappeared after we sprayed insecticide together and hosed the place down. However, no one could tell what tomorrow would bring. My brother Fruits said: I bet there'll be rats tomorrow. And civet cats the day after tomorrow. And porcupines the day after that. And then leopards. And finally dinosaurs.

We had so much rubbish every day I thought the rubbish collection man would refuse to collect it anymore, but he just said:

— Nice rooftop

— You can turn it into a garden

Dear neighbours, I have told you all that has happened. What I would like to tell you is that there were so many bugs on the wall we might have missed out on a couple of them. If that was the case, they could have climbed into your window and gone into your kitchen. So you must check your pots and pans when you have dinner tonight, or else you might let the bugs get into your tummies.

I have showed this letter to my aunt Liberty. She said that I got the word "ironing-board" wrong; I spelt it "broad". That was of course a mistake, and I corrected it. My aunt Liberty said —

and my brother Fruits too, and me, too — we're sorry we can't make nice flowers grow on your wall, and we're sorry it's not possible for you to pick a pear or something just by stretching your hands out of the window. We'll try to think of a way. With best wishes,

Yours Cordially,

Braids

 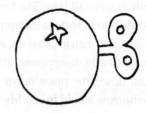

6

Here are some photos I want to show you.

1. In this photo we can see a hobby horse. The hobby horses we usually see look like rocking chairs, but this one looks like a sausage dog. It has a red head, and a green body that is the length of a bench. The photo depicts a corner of a park. The horse is, of course, in the park. Besides the horse, the park also boasts swings, slides, a climbing frame, and a sandpit. A group of kids are gathered around the sandpit, making sand cakes and sand biscuits. Opposite the sandpit is a roundabout. If you stand on it for a long time, you'll feel dizzy.

There are park benches near the swings and the slides. All the benches used to be green in colour, but after a while they got tired of being the same colour. Some became orange benches, some egg-yoke benches, some strawberry benches. Still, there were a couple which continued the long, green tradition.

Since this park with its red-headed hobby horse is in fact a very small park, the name printed on its ID card is Public Garden. Sometimes it's also called Playground, at other times, City Lung. There are many lungs in this city; some are good and some not so good. The not-so-good lungs look like this: no trees, no grass, only mesh wire as far as the eye can see. The good lungs are much easier on the eye. There are shrubs along their borders, and

ponds for toy boats. Even the flower beds show interesting differences. For instance, the one in which small shrubs and flowering plants are growing is a specimen bed; the one in which a huge variety of flowers is planted is a bushy bed. In most of the good lungs there are squat stone chairs of various designs; they all look like sculptures.

The man standing next to the hobby horse is Merry Mak. As the photo was taken in winter, Merry Mak is wearing a black uniform and a hat in it. Merry Mak, so dressed, may give the impression that he was a policeman, but in fact he was just a park warden. The stick he is holding in his hand is of course not a truncheon. At one end of the stick there is a long spike for picking up wastepaper from the ground. Every day Merry Mak picked up wastepaper in his little park. He also had to see to it that the hobby horse did not go hungry, and that no cactus suddenly sprouted from the sandpit. It goes without saying that Merry Mak had to make sure that park benches did not grow too fond of wet paint.

The small public gardens are usually in the care of one person, and at that time Merry Mak was taking care of just such a garden. Though these gardens are small, they all have a pavilion, and in one of the pavilion walls there is always a door. Behind that door are stored all things necessary for the management of the garden. If at times Merry Mak was nowhere to be seen in the garden, that was because he was behind the door. But such times were rare. Would staring at a few mops for a long time make Merry Mak truly merry? In those days Merry Mak used to stand at the garden entrance talking to the ice-cream pedlar. He sometimes said: How come there aren't any almonds in your almond ice-cream? If it goes on like this you might as well sell iced milk. But he did not really say this very often. After all, he didn't really stand at the garden entrance all day long.

I just said that Merry Mak had a lot of work to do, such as checking whether the hobby horse still had its tail intact, or whether camels had been strolling over the sandpit, so there was no reason why he should stand at the garden entrance all day long. Merry Mak was always kept busy in the garden: he had to take care of the garden, and he had to take care of the children in it, not to mention the children's grannies, and the grannies' daughters. Just to give you an example, once a child's mother was attacked by a whole hive of bees because she had sprayed her hair. Merry Mak had to come to her rescue, with the result that his hands were stung in quite a few places. As there was no ointment he could use, Merry Mak covered his hands in soap suds.

Just then a City Grooming Official came by and saw Merry Mak. He shook his head and said: Well, well, and what do you think you're doing? If you want to blow bubbles you've got to use your mouth, not your hands.

2. Though there is a grassy area in the centre of this photo, that is not a park; it is a football stadium. The man who is sitting on the steps is Merry Mak. After he had worked in the Public Garden for a while, Merry Mak was transferred here. Since this is a big football stadium, there are more visitors here than at the garden, and the place is much more lively. On match days, the dozen entrances to the stadium are opened wide, and crowds rush in as though they are invading a walled city. The stands on all sides are filled in no time. And if it rains, then the stands are filled with umbrellas and newspapers. There are as many people outside the football stadium as there are inside, and they all talk at the top of their voices, like a thousand kettles boiling at the same time. At one corner of the field there is a huge steel structure, and the big clock on top of it looks as though it, too, is cooking something. In shape, it is less like a kettle or a thermos, than a pressure cooker.

During football matches Merry Mak had little to do, so he would sit down and watch the game. Sometimes he sat on the turf, at other times behind the goal. Occasionally, a football would fly his way, almost knocking a reporter's camera out of his hands before skimming his head to land somewhere behind him. Merry Mak always hurried off to pick up the ball and kick it back in front of the thousands of pairs of eyes. He felt he was exactly like Pele, the Brazilian footballer. However, the goalkeeper caught the ball with perfect ease every time.

Things which Merry Mak had never witnessed before would often occur during football matches. Once, for instance, there were these two teams on the field, one wearing red, the other white. Within three minutes of the match starting, the red team was awarded six penalty kicks. Thereupon, the spectators on the stands suddenly turned themselves into gongs, each making an earth-shattering noise. And then a large number of tomatoes flew out from the stands: even now, Merry Mak still hasn't figured out where all those tomatoes came from. Anyway, the tomatoes all landed in the centre of the football field, turning the white team red. That put an end to the match.

When everyone started throwing tomatoes onto the field, Merry Mak found that he, too, had five tomatoes in his hands. He yelled and threw them all out. Merry Mak found out the price of throwing five tomatoes afterwards: he spent five hours sweeping up crushed tomatoes on the football field. The moral of this story is: tomatocs are best eaten at home.

Then there was this football team. The name of the team was Foul Play. They won every match they played, yet technically they were not that brilliant. Since Merry Mak had watched so many football matches, he could tell real technique from nasty tricks. Every time this team played a match, its members kicked and hit their opposite numbers, and when the referee's back was turned, they shoved their opponents to the ground, or caught the ball with their hands, or attacked their opponents with their teeth. Once they even kidnapped the other side's goalkeeper, and sent on an imposter from their own team. That being the case, of course they won. The teams that played against them were Gentlemen Teams and Righteous Teams that all played by the book, and so these teams lost every time. You would think that members of Foul Play would be ashamed of themselves. But there you're wrong: they actually behaved as though playing foul was the most glorious thing to do, and as soon as they stepped onto the football field they looked on themselves as heroes. What really sickened Merry Mak was that the whole team made it on the footballers' honours list, every single one of them.

There was of course a lot more that went on in the stadium, but since Merry Mak is not interested in publishing the memoirs of his football-field days, these two anecdotes should suffice.

3. In this photo Merry Mak is standing at the back of a pavilion. It being summer, he was wearing a short-sleeved yellow cotton uniform. Merry Mak wasn't wearing a hat this time round; the hat was optional, and he decided not to wear it in that heat. This time Merry Mak wasn't holding a truncheon in his hand either. That was because the new regulations governing park wardens said that they did not have to pick up wastepaper with a nail on a stick anymore. In fact, since the Clean City Campaign was launched, the wastepaper in the park all gathered itself into the rubbish bins. That is something which deserves a thumbs-up.

The Merry Mak in the photo is standing at the back of a pavilion. More accurately, he is standing by the side of a few pots of chilies — presents from Silly Gardener to Merry Mak. Three pots were red-hot chilies, while two were sweet chilies. Every day Merry Mak came round ten times to check on them. Since chilies like it mild and humid, Merry Mak was concerned that they would come down with fever from the heat and the fierce sun, or they might stop breathing because of too much rain. Every day, Merry Mak came to prune their branches, cut off new shoots, catch red spiders, and put straw in the pot to prevent the chilies from rotting should they come into contact with the soil. Because of the care he lavished on them, the chilies called a meeting and decided that they had to repay his kindness.

But Merry Mak did not eat any chilies. As he had more and more of them, he strung them together and hung them on a wall at home. Someone said:

— hanging chilies on the wall

— for fear of the vampire

It was Merry Mak's neighbour who said this. He was fond of reading horror stories in bed, so he frequently came to borrow Merry Mak's flashlight. Recently, due to a lack of burial space, this city started advocating cremation. Merry Mak's neighbour, being a good citizen, expressed his support for this by sending his opinion to the collection box at the Government Secretariat. His opinion: Cremation can put an end to vampires. The idea came to him after he saw the chilies on Merry Mak's wall.

Merry Mak had another neighbour; this one was fond of reading detective stories in the early mornings. He frequently came to borrow Merry Mak's mackintosh, and when he saw the chilies on Merry Mak's wall, he took a string back for analysis. Some time later he gave Merry Mak a report in which he pointed out that chilies were originally grown in South America and were introduced in the fifteenth or sixteenth century to Europe from where the Portuguese took them to India in the sixteenth century, after which they were introduced from India to China at the end of the Ming dynasty (i.e. in the seventeenth century). The report also indicated that chilies belong to the Solanaceae family, same as taro, tobacco and tomato. Naturally Merry Mak knew nothing about all this. He couldn't care less what family chilies belong to, or whether they're from South America or South Africa. All he knew was: either you don't grow them, or you grow them well. Make the chilies happy, make the chilies healthy.

Merry Mak didn't eat chilies, but there was one time when he ate two. It happened like this: Merry Mak lived in this high-rise building which housed a lot of people. He lived on the top floor, and every day he had to take the lift several times.

One day, as Merry Mak walked through the main entrance of the building, he saw the doors of the lift closing slowly. He thought that if he ran fast, he would probably make it, and so he barged into the lift. Now there were five or six people in the lift, men and women, old and young. As soon as they saw Merry Mak barge in like this, in his jeans, faded shirt and long hair, they pushed the STOP button, and then they pushed OPEN, and then they all walked out, leaving Merry Mak alone in the lift.

— my hair's just a bit long
— but I'm a good guy

Merry Mak shouted to them. However, they all returned him a vote of no confidence. Merry Mak put up his hands high above his head and turned around once, showing them that he was not armed with anything like a knife or toy gun or what not, but they still showed no confidence in him. Merry Mak thought of coming out of the lift so that they could go up first, but then if he did that, the others would probably think he was up to some trick, and so he took the lift alone and got home.

When he got home, Merry Mak was far from merry. What had happened to this world? My hair's just a bit long, he said, but I'm not a bad guy. Yet he could not really blame his neighbours in the lift. Were he to cut his hair, wear a suit and a tie — but come what may, *that* is one thing Merry Mak would never do.

He brooded on it for a good part of the day, and the longer he brooded, the less merry he became. He blurted out: Might as well put an end to it all and turn myself into air or something. And true to his words, he immediately banged his head against the wall. As he did so, however, he bumped his head right into a string of chilies, two of which were flattened and fell into his mouth. The chilies were *so* hot that tears came out of his eyes. But the tears also washed Merry Mak's unhappiness away.

After that, Merry Mak always walked slowly to the lift; he also said good morning and good afternoon to the people he came across in the building, so people decided to take the lift with him. And after that, every time Merry Mak's friends were unhappy, he gave them a string of chilies. That way, his home was saved from turning into a chilies barn.

4. This is a photo of a park entrance. Park entrances look different in different cities, and the ones in this city are no exception; they are alike and yet unalike.

Some park entrances are like this: Two stone lions, one sitting on either side. There is a cub under the foot of one lion, and a ball under the foot of the other. There are no lions at the park entrance in this photo; all the lions have gone on sentry duty outside banks and department stores.

At some park entrances there is a wooden signboard with a tourist map featuring all sorts of arrows. They point: this way to the dolphin theatre, that way to the elephants, this way to scrambled eggs. They also say: you are here. There is no signboard at the park entrance in the photo; all the signboards have gone to shopping arcades and high-rise buildings.

Some park entrances are like the ferry pier: there's a turnstile; or they are like cinemas: you go to a little window first, to buy a ticket. There is no box office at the park entrance in this photo. That's why it's a lovely park. Whoever feels like it can go in and out three hundred times a day, empty-handed.

Some park entrances are distinctly peculiar: when you look at it from the outside, you simply cannot tell that it is a park entrance. It's just a tiny door, surrounded by black-tiled whitewashed walls. If you look at it from an angle, you see the twisted-rope patterns formed by the tiles. But when you walk through the door, everything is different. All of a sudden you meet a big garden with hills, pools, pillars, pavilions and pagodas. You walk for a while and come to another tiny door, behind which is another big garden, totally different from the one before. There are fish ponds, winding bridges, and lily ponds with flowers stretching out their long arms or sleeping quietly on the water. These gardens are all linked together; you cannot tell how many there are.

The park in this photo is not like that. Its door is wide open. What surrounds the park is mesh wire. The contents of this park are very transparent.

Some parks have their names written at the entrance. They say: I'm Botanical Garden; I'm Birds Garden. The park in this photo has this written at its entrance: Happy Prince Garden. Beside the name there is a signboard detailing the rules of the park. Most park rules are like this:

A. No beating trees

B. No maltreating hobby horses

C. No scolding park benches

D. No making faces at park rules

Etcetera. And also, No picking fruits and flowers; No climbing over walls and railings; No cycling. And also, Cats not allowed. Merry Mak knew all these rules by heart, and knew them well. If someone took off his shoes and walked into the pond, he'd recite: No catching fish in the park. If someone was lying on a park bench after midnight, he'd recite: No sleeping in the park at night.

At first Merry Mak couldn't remember the rules, so he copied them into a small notebook and read them aloud all day, even when he was walking and eating. Soon he knew them by heart. Even in his dreams he would stand at the park entrance and read the rules over and over again. One night, he had a dream, and of course he was reading out park rules. But that park was really strange, because there was just one rule. It said: Yellow people, green dogs, not allowed.[1] Merry Mak was furious when he saw it, so furious that even two strings of chilies did not cure him. And so he cut down the rules with an axe and ground them into powder. He then mixed the powder with well water and drank it. That quenched his fury a bit. Merry Mak then put up a signboard of his own. It said: Free tea and coffee available. Merry Mak said that in the future parks would all be like that.

In this photo Merry Mak is standing under the bronze statue of the Happy Prince. The park is called Happy Prince Garden because of this statue. Some people may ask: Is there a swallow at its feet? As for that, you better ask Happy Prince himself.

— I see swallows

— I also see wild ducks and kites

says Happy Prince.

With the passing of March every year, migratory birds come to this city. Some just pass through, others stay for the winter. They come in flocks, flying along rivers and coastlines. Most of the migratory birds travel at night, when lighthouses and lights along the coast direct their wings. But the swallows like travelling in the daytime. They follow the shores of the city harbour and circle the low lying areas. One or two would

---

[1] This is an allusion to a signboard at the entrance to a park in a Shanghai foreign concession in the 1930s and 1940s: Chinese and dogs not allowed.

alight on the shoulders of the Happy Prince statue.

— how long are you going to stay

— what is it like out there

The Prince always asks.

Swallow had decided not to tell Happy Prince about the outside world. The next day, Swallow left. It circled the Happy Prince statue once and then followed the other swallows to another place. In this city, there are fewer and fewer eaves where the swallows can nest. As for the wild ducks which stay at the estuary, they never come to the park. They just fly along the river, and when they reach this city, they stay in the bay where river water merges with sea water. They used to gather in Plover Bay sometimes, but that bay has been turned into a reservoir, and the migratory birds have to look for somewhere else to stay. Should Happy Prince without his swallow still be called Happy Prince?

5. This photo is only remotely connected to the park. It was lying together with a notebook on a park bench, probably left there by a young man. Merry Mak saw them and picked them up, hoping that someone would come to look for them, but no one did.

The man in the photo is wearing a cap, with one eye covered with a piece of black cloth. According to the notebook this man was a film director. The person who made the notes knew everything about the life and works of this director. From the well-organized material in the notebook one could tell that this person had great admiration for the director. He called him a recreator of Western heroes and his films Western epics and pastorals.

Merry Mak had no intention of reading what was in the notebook. He knew perfectly well that reading someone else's documents was a very impolite thing to do. The fact that he opened it was only because he wanted to see if there were any names inside. Merry Mak thought that it was probably a student's notebook with the teacher's explication of lessons all written down. Wouldn't it be terrible to lose this? Merry Mak also thought that he might find the name of the school or other clues inside.

That's why he opened the notebook. He found nothing. Only the photo fell out of it, the photo of the film director wearing a cap.

Merry Mak could not understand why the person who lost the notebook did not come to look for it. The notes were so well-organized, they could not have been compiled in a day or two, or even a week or two. Such a detailed record and so much information — the person who wrote it must have spent a long time collecting material. He must have read many books and articles by this director. He must have seen all his films countless times.

Silly Gardener said: This person had probably been to a number of places that day, like the library, the cinema, school, a restaurant, walking down the street, or riding on buses and ferries. He may not remember where he left his notebook. Then he said: Why don't you place an ad in the papers. As he said this he took a few coins out of his pocket, and Merry Mak did the same. After drawing toothpicks, it was decided that Merry Mak would take responsibility for this. Merry Mak wrote out a classified ad — four large words and twenty small ones — and placed it with a newspaper to run for two days. The ad read like this:

Film Director's Notebook Found

If you have lost a one-eyed becapped Director's Notebook please come to Happy Prince Garden for it No reward expected

Since the words Happy Prince Garden appeared in the papers, people naturally wanted to find out who had done it. Auntie Phoenix, one of the park toilet cleaners, soon learned the truth. She commented: The cost of the ad would pay for lunch for two. Merry Mak and Silly Gardener probably didn't want their meals anymore. Auntie Rainbow, the other toilet cleaner, said: They should have asked for a fifty-dollar reward. Some other people expressed a different opinion: They should have put that money into our pool for the quinella and the six-up.[2]

A few weeks passed after the ad appeared in the newspaper, during which no one came to ask about the director's notebook. Silly Gardener

---

[2] Different ways of betting on horses.

and Merry Mak were of course very much disappointed. Silly Gardener said: The ad only ran for two days, maybe he didn't see it. It always happens this way: those who are involved don't see it, and those who aren't do. Since Silly Gardener and Merry Mak did not have the money to place any more ads, they could only keep the notebook. Had Merry Mak turned to the notebook's last page instead of the first, he would have seen this line:

He has butchered more Indians than all the famous cavalry generals put together. It is precisely because his technique is so beautiful and refined that I feel so sad.

6. That man sat silently on a rock. He did not walk around in the park, and he did not notice the difference between this park and other parks.

That man sitting on the rock, what was he doing in the park? He paid no notice to the flowers around him. This was the best season for flowers. Next to the rock he was occupying there were two canopy flowers and two scribbling flowers. But it was still the azaleas which dominated the scene — purple, red and pink, like a tapestry hanging on the slope. Yet the man sitting on the rock took absolutely no notice of the flowers. After having sat there for a while, he stood up, and he actually stood on the rock. As soon as he got up there he started talking, and the more he talked the more excited he became. Unfortunately, at that time a band was playing in the centre of the park, and everyone gathered around the music.

Merry Mak was walking round the park on his own. When he came to a rock he saw someone standing on it practising public speaking, but there was no audience. Seeing how excited the speaker was, he stood there to listen. It turned out that the man wanted to be a president. He said:

Verily I say to you: You can practise population control; you can decrease the number of your descendants. The result of this will be that you will become a minority. As for us, we will do just the opposite. We will let our descendants be fertile; their number will exceed that of stars in the sky and grains of sand on the earth. Many, many years from now, our descendants will be the majority of the human race. When election day comes, we will win. We will be MPs; we will be presidents.

The speaker was weeping buckets of tears as he talked. Merry Mak was totally engrossed. Suddenly, the other park warden came over, saw this man, and told him not to speechify on a rock.

— this is a park

— no advertising toothpaste here

said the warden. The man on the rock had come to the end of his speech anyway. He jumped down, nodded to Merry Mak, who was his whole audience, and left.

After the man had left, the park warden said to Merry Mak: What kind of a warden are you? How could you allow someone to advertise toothpaste in a park? After this, the man submitted a report to the city administration official. As Merry Mak had made several mistakes before, and now there was an official report against him, he lost his job. The mistakes he had made included:

A. Blowing bubbles in the park

B. Throwing tomatoes in the football stadium

C. Permitting pedlars to advertise in the park

There were several other exciting events which took place in the park, but since Merry Mak had left by then, he did not witness them. One of these was that time when a lot of people squabbled for a place to fish on the concrete platform in the middle of the fountain.

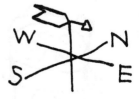

7

The man who is checking out a door, peering and knocking at it, is North. He is conducting a physical for the door. It's a wooden door. As the weather has turned warm, North has to check whether the door is behaving like a fat caterpillar whose body undergoes sudden expansion. He gets hold of a ruler and measures the door's width and then its length. The door seems stable, not showing any changes. North is satisfied.

— you see, when you make a door

— the first thing is to choose well-seasoned wood

North says to himself. When North wants to make a door, he gets hold of the best quality wood and then seasons it until it is as dry as the autumn weather before he fashions a door out of it. On the ground floor of the big house that is No. 1 Hobby Horse Road, there is this room with a coal stove in the centre and planks lining its walls. North comes to light the stove regularly. That is how he seasons the wood he uses for making doors.

To begin with North was a carpenter's apprentice. His teacher had several apprentices, among whom North was the first. Altogether, he spent four years under his teacher. In the first year, he swept the floor, took out the rubbish, and went with his teacher to buy raw material. When his teacher took a rest, he gathered up the tools and counted the pieces of wood. Around that time one of North's fellow apprentices said: How come we haven't learned a thing? Why

doesn't he teach us how to make bunk beds? North said nothing. When the teacher was making windows, he watched carefully and tried hard to remember everything. Now he knew roughly how a window should be made.

In the second year, the teacher told everyone to sharpen drawknives and chisels. He even told them to sharpen the saws with an iron file. Another of North's fellow apprentices said: We've come to learn carpentry, not knife-sharpening. The one who said this did not finish his apprenticeship. He eventually ended up as a knife-sharpener, going round the streets to sharpen kitchen knives and scissors.

In the third year, the teacher told his apprentices to make stools or drawers. North did his own measurements, cut the wood and, following his teacher's usual routine, worked at the drawers carefully. There were a couple of times when the tenon joints did not match and the drawers turned out lop-sided. Yet after a year's work, North made very good drawers.

In the fourth year, the teacher told them to make whole pieces of furniture. During this year North really gave his all to the solid tables, chairs, doors and windows that he made. The teacher nodded his head in approval. In those four years, the teacher had taken on many outside jobs such as making doors and windows for new flats and wall units for nice rooms. North paid attention to how all this was done, and learned the trade.

Since North spent considerable time with plasterers and painters, and also had his meals with them, he often asked them about how to paint a door well and how to mend cracks in a wall. Everyone was willing to teach him, so North learned to paint and plaster as well.

At the end of the four years, the apprentices all went off on their own. North opened a small shop. He made some tables and chairs, and lots of doors. People came occasionally to buy the tables and chairs, but no one ever bought a door. The doors stayed boringly in the shop, looking like paintings without lines or colour. North's shop resembled an exhibition hall of blank paintings.

East was North's fellow apprentice and somewhat younger than him. He only completed his apprenticeship one year after North did, but he was very clever. When he left the teacher, East also opened a shop. He did not make any doors, just tables, chairs and cabinets. He did not use the hand saw either, he used electric ones. In this way he was able to make lots and lots of tables and chairs, and his business boomed.

One day East paid North a visit. North was making a chair. He was so careful going about it that you'd think the chair was a work of art meant for the museum. He took his time, carefully marking the details as he worked. And so East told North: Why bother doing it by hand? Buy some machines, work more quickly, produce more goods. He also said: There's no harm in skimping a bit in places where people can't see. That way you'll make a lot more money and open a bigger shop. East also said that he could lend North some money so he could buy machines. North thought about it, but decided that hand-made tables and chairs had a better feel to them, just like hand-knitted jumpers.

There was another fellow apprentice who came to their teacher not because he wanted to be a carpenter, but because he wanted to be a poet. He told himself: Writing poems is the same as making chairs. After four years with the teacher, he, too, finished his apprenticeship. The teacher naturally did not teach him how to write poetry, or what books he could read to learn the craft of poetry, because the teacher himself never wrote any poetry. This apprentice, however, said that he had learned a lot and now he knew how to write poetry. First you sweep the floor, then you take out the rubbish, and then you go with the teacher to buy raw material. This means: read, and experience. Then it was sharpening chisels and filing saws, which means polish your language. Finally, making tables, chairs and drawers, meaning, write, and write.

This poet-apprentice visited North very often, and every time he went North was looking at his doors. He thought that North made excellent doors, even better than the teacher did. And so he was the only one who ever went to look at North's doors. At long last, North's doors had found a true friend who appreciated their worth.

One day, North was sitting in his shop, looking at the doors he had made. Why do people only come for tables and chairs? Why don't they buy doors? Doors can be hung on the wall; you can pin all sorts of pictures on them; doors can be used as a sitting mat on the floor.

North starved for some days, looking at his doors. Then he abruptly closed his shop. The next day, he came to No. 1 Hobby Horse Road to become the doorman. That was many years ago.

— mind the doors

the water-lilies' father said.

— yes, I will

said North. And so North carried out his duty diligently by minding the doors of No. 1 Hobby Horse Road, all seventeen of them. Every morning, when North got up, he checked on the doors one by one, watching out for rust on the locks and the tension of the springs. Every evening, North went the rounds again, paying special attention to the doors that led to the rooftop because they bordered on the outside world. At night, North was the one who bolted all the doors. The water-lilies' father was very satisfied with North's work.

During the war, the water-lilies and their father moved somewhere else. North did not go with them. He stayed behind with his wife to mind the doors — Has this door been eaten by termites? Has a crack appeared on this door because of the bombing? And so the doors all stayed healthy. The bombs never caused any cracks to appear on the doors, but that year they did cause a gaping hole to appear on the head of North's wife. Later, after the war was over, the water-lilies moved back to the big house. They had lost their father, and North had lost his wife, but the doors were all right. A long time after that, the water-lilies went away again.

— mind the doors

the water-lilies said.

— yes, I will

said North. And so the water-lilies went away in a mechanical bird, leaving behind them this nest which according to them is like ninth-grade *longjing* tea in the chrysanthemum season. On the first floor now lives

Braids, who is fond of sharpening pencils, and Fruits, who is fond of
singing "bake some bread, bake some bread, it sure tastes good" on the
stairs, and their mother.

Every day, North still goes the rounds to check on the seventeen
doors, and at night he carefully bolts the doors leading to the rooftop and
the skywell. As for the front door, he never forgets to check that all five
padlocks are there.

Besides checking on the doors twice a day, North spends his time
making doors in the big room. When North is carefully checking on the
doors, he occasionally finds one among the seventeen that is too old, or
whose paint is falling off. Then he goes to light the stove for seasoning
wood to make the planks even drier. And then he makes a door. That's a
bedroom, so let's make a cross-framed door. So saying, North takes the
planks and posts to the big room. Next to the staircase on the ground floor
of this house, there is a door opening into a very big room. Every time
Fruits goes up or down the stairs he hears the sound of wood-sawing or
wood-planing. The door is only half-closed, but because the room is so
big, he can't see the person inside. Yet Fruits knows that North must be
in there. At this time North is designing his door — six feet by three feet.
He takes up a piece of dark-coloured pencil the shape of a somewhat flat
egg, puts the tip in his mouth, moistens it with his spittle and makes some
marks on the wood. He then marks out the position for the mortise and
tenon, puts the wood on a trestle and starts sawing. North's hair has turned
grey. When other people's hair turns grey they say:

— my back is so stiff

— my bones are aching so

— I can't thread a needle anymore

However, North's back is not stiff, his bones don't ache, and although
he doesn't have to thread a needle, if it was required of him, he wouldn't
need to wear glasses to do it. Though his hair has turned grey, North still
walks briskly, his stride firm and his body bolt upright. When he planes
wood his movements are still powerful. When North decides to make a
door, it usually takes several months. He likes to work slowly, that was

true even when his hair was jet black. He likes to work slowly, treating every door like a sculpture, a work of art. There are seventeen doors in this house, and these doors have to be replaced once every few years. This year it is the turn of Room One on the first floor and Room Two on the ground floor. Next year it will be the turn of the rooftop door and the skywell door, while last year it was the kitchen door and the bathroom door. The water-lilies' father said, mind the doors. He never came to see North make doors, nor did the water-lilies. North was always alone in the big room, shaving wood, fixing the joints, varnishing the doors. However, the day came when someone walked into North's world.

It happened when North was priming the cross-framed door. A little girl stood at his door, and North knew that she was Braids. He rested his gloved hand on the tilting door. Braids smiled at him, and he smiled back.

— What are you doing?

Braids asked. North beckoned to her, and she came into the room and stood in front of him. Braids could see that North was making a door. She also noticed the brown powder in the bucket; it looked like sesame paste. North told her that he was making a door, and he needed to put a layer of primer on it to fill in the air holes in the wood. Braids watched as North worked on the door, and asked him whether it was very heavy, and whether planing wood was very hard work. She stayed there until her alarm clock rang, at which point she had to say goodbye, with the promise that she would come back later.

A few days later, another person came into North's world. This time it was Fruits. He brought with him two rice dumplings for North, and he also stayed on to watch him work on the door. And so North made some friends. What is more, North didn't have to go out for his meals anymore: now Fruits and Braids came down each day to take him upstairs for lunch and dinner; they also brought him his breakfast and tea.

One day North stopped working on his door. He put it aside and started to make a ping-pong table. Now the ping-pong table is standing in another big room on the ground floor.

This day, Liberty comes to North's workshop. She has come with
Braids.

— this is Uncle from downstairs
— this is my aunt Liberty

says Braids. North is just drilling the holes for the door hinges. He
says: So, yet another spectator. Next time I'll charge an entrance fee. So
saying he stands up. He has been working for a good half-day, and it is
time for him to take a break. He stands up and stretches himself. There
are no chairs or stools in this big room. He clears the wood shavings off
a pile of something and sits down. He says to Liberty: If you don't mind
the mess, just sit where you like.

Liberty follows his example, walks over to another pile of something,
and sweeps the wood shavings away. As she does so, she notices that
what lies under the wood is in fact a pile of books, with the spines all
facing the wall and the edges all turned the colour of wood. Liberty picks
up one volume: *Records of the Grand Historian*. Liberty looks at several
other volumes: *Records of the Grand Historian*. It turns out that this pile
consists of *Records of the Grand Historian, History of the Han Dynasty,
History of the Later Han Dynasty*, and *History of the Three Kingdoms*.

— are you sitting on books as well, sir

Liberty asks as she walks briskly over to North. North replies: Why,
yes, and stands up. Liberty picks up one of the books and flips through
it. It turns out to be *Comprehensive Mirror of Government*.

— these are all very good books

says Liberty.

— how come they're lying around on the ground

asks Liberty.

And so North provides an answer the content of which includes three
points:

    1. there are no chairs in the room

    2. they do not serve any other purpose

    3. there are so many of them

After his simple summary, North goes on to explain in greater detail the point about "there are no chairs in the room":

Once upon a time, North felt tired when he was working. That was because he was down with the flu, and after working for a while, he felt like sitting down. Yet there were no chairs in the room. At that point, he saw the books on the shelves, so he took a few piles and put them on the ground to serve as stools. Sitting on books is quite comfortable, he says.

There really are no chairs in this big room. The room is as spacious as a basketball court, its four walls lined with large planks of wood which completely cover the walls. As a result, the room looks like it is roughly partitioned off with planks. At this moment, in one corner of the centre of the room stands a trestle, and there are wood shavings lying on a floor of sawdust.

Liberty notices that there are also blocks of wood of various shapes and sizes on the floor, as well as hammers, nails and a saw. Why doesn't North make himself a few chairs? Liberty wonders. After all, he's a carpenter. North shakes his head at the thought of chairs. He says he has come to No. 1 Hobby Horse Road to mind the doors, not to make chairs.

As for the point "they do not serve any other purpose", North explains as follows: You've seen the piano upstairs, haven't you? No one ever plays that piano. North doesn't know why that is the case, but he remembers that on the day it was delivered he eagerly unlocked all the padlocks on the main door and pulled it wide open, and then he watched seven or eight men carry the piano into the house. It was wrapped up in sacks. Out of the wrapping protruded two jet black wooden legs, and several glittering things. A huge crowd gathered outside the door. Everyone hazarded a guess:

— looks like a desk

— looks like a fat foreign chair

This mysterious object was soon put into the sitting room upstairs where it turned dumb. If it hadn't been for the person who came on the day of its delivery to touch it here and press it there, making a series of tinkling noises, North would never have known that it was a piano. Since

then, this piano had never made a sound. However, North had heard the
water-lilies say:

— even the orchids don't have one

— and we've got one

It was said that the orchids had a lot of books at home, and that they
loved reading. The water-lilies didn't. When North first came to No.1
Hobby Horse Road to mind the doors, there were also many books in the
big room downstairs. The door leading to the big room was shut most of
the time, and no one ever went in. Occasionally, when a couple of guests
came to visit, everyone might go in together to have a look here and a
look there, but they all came out pretty quickly.

As far as North remembers, the water-lilies' father never read, nor
did the water-lilies. That is why North has drawn this conclusion: They
do not serve any other purpose. North figured that since the rows and rows
of books lining the shelves were absolutely no use, he might as well take
a few piles down to serve as a stool. That way they'd at least be of some
use. And that was what he did.

As for "there are so many of them", North explains as follows:

There are so many books on the shelves, what's wrong with taking
some down here? So saying, he removes one plank after another, until the
wall behind the planks emerges.

There is no wall behind the planks, just bookshelves. North points to
two of the other walls, saying: In this room, the walls are covered with
bookshelves. He remembers the water-lilies saying: We've got far more
books than the orchids.

— you see, *so* many books

— what's wrong with taking some down here

says North. Liberty stands dazed. So there are bookshelves behind
all these planks, and the shelves are full of books! Liberty steps over the
planks, wood shavings, and sawdust, and stands in front of the bookshelves. She lifts her hand to touch one book after another, and a shower
of dust falls down from them. The books on the shelves are very old; they
are beautiful editions. Yet the people who owned these beautiful good

books did not even take one look at them.

— I'd like to come and read these books

— may I

Liberty feels that her voice is in need of Beauty Candy. North nods his approval, saying that if it suits her, she can read here twenty-four hours a day. But she is not to take the books out of the room, she'd have to read here. The books belong to the water-lilies, and North's responsibility is to mind of the doors for them, which means that with the exception of people, anything inside a door must not get out.

Liberty stands rooted in front of the bookshelves, not knowing which book to pick first. When she sees that there are actually picture books as well, it becomes even more difficult for her to tear herself away.

— it's just impossible

— why didn't anyone read them

Liberty says as she shakes her head in disbelief, and shakes it again.

— well, someone did

says North. He remembers the poet-apprentice. One day the poet-apprentice came to see North. No. 1 Hobby Horse Road was quite empty at that time because the water-lilies' father left after saying "Mind the doors well" to seek safety in a small village. That was during the war.

That day, North was making a door, as usual, and there were several piles of books serving as stools on the floor. When the poet-apprentice came, he sat down on the books. When he saw that the pile consisted of *Records of the Grand Historian* and *History of the Three Kingdoms* he also said something to the effect of "such good books", after which he sighed: What a pity that I don't have the time to read them properly.

North could not read. He asked the poet-apprentice what the books were about, and poet-apprentice said they were all about emperors. Some emperors were good, others bad. It is true that whether they were good or bad, all emperors had to die, but good ones gave numerous people a happy life, and bad ones made thousands and millions suffer. North knew nothing about books, and he knew nothing about emperors, he only knew

how to mind the doors. The poet-apprentice said: Making doors is in fact
the same as being emperor.

After saying farewell to North, the poet-apprentice also went to mind
a door, but that door was a bit different from North's doors. North takes
care of the doors in the water-lilies' house in No. 1 Hobby Horse Road;
the door which the poet-apprentice went to guard was shapeless, a huge
abstract door.

As North looks at Liberty shaking her head in front of the bookshelves, he seems to see the poet-apprentice. But the image just flashes
by and disappears. As Liberty stands in front of the bookshelves, she hears
the books talking.

— looks like the place will liven up
  says one book.
— end of a hundred years of solitude
  says another.

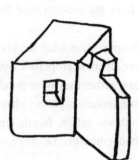

8

I am drawing a chart on a blank sheet of paper. No one has told me to do it; I just want to do it. I've always been like this: as soon as I see a blackboard, I take out a few sheets of paper to doodle on.

That's right, there is a blackboard in front of me, which means I am sitting in a classroom again. Today there are quite a number of people in this classroom, older ones as well as young ones, tie-wearers as well as denim-wearers, and also girls wearing plenty of sun-tan oil. We have come from all four corners of the city; we have never met before; we all walked into the classroom alone, picked out an empty chair, and sat down. Soon after everyone had settled down, in came someone who preferred to stand.

— good morning
— welcome to the Telephone Company

he said. He did not close the door, he even opened all the windows. Obviously he likes fresh air. So do we.

— we are very happy
— that you have decided to work for us

he said. From the way he looked, I figured he was an engineer.

He said: We have asked you to come here today because we would like to tell you briefly about the structure of our company so that you will know a little about it. Having said this, he proceeded step by step, beginning with the structure of the board of

directors. And I proceeded to draw a chart on a blank sheet of paper. Occasionally I put in one or two objects which look like telephones. My chart looks like an upside-down tree; it also looks like the picture of the nerves man I saw in Horns Medical Centre recently; it also looks like a river with many tributaries. At the head of the chart I have listed the position of various people:

> Chief Engineer
>
> Assistant Chief Engineer
>
> Executive Engineer

At this point I made a quick sketch of a telephone handset. I took a good look at it for quite a while, and it occurred to me that the telephone handset is very much like a human ear. Oh, that's it: someone else had said as much. There was this man who couldn't hear anyone talking to him from the floor above; he couldn't hear people calling out his name in the street; he couldn't hear anyone who had gone on a trip tell him how beautiful the scenery was. However, after the arrival of the telephone, he heard everything. That was why he said the telephone was in fact an ear.

> Senior Engineers
>
> Engineers
>
> Assistant Engineering Supervisors

I added a few rows to the chart. I also added a telephone line to the handset.

As soon as a telephone line is installed, the telephone is linked up with the outside world. And so the police station says: Dial 999. And the ICAC[1] says: Please call 266366.

One telephone line goes like this: Hello, is that Flower? A bunch of us are going for a swim, why don't you come along? Three-thirty this afternoon at the railway station side of Ding-dong pier.[2] And so Flower

---

[1] The Independent Commission Against Corruption, answerable directly to the Governor of Hong Kong, was set up in the early 1970s. Ever since its inception it has run a highly successful community relations campaign.

[2] Before the Kowloon-Canton Railway terminus was moved to Honghom, it was situated in Tsimshatsui, next to the Star Ferry. Now only the old clock tower remains.

goes swimming with a group of friends.

Another telephone line goes like this: Oh, you're seventeen this year, and you don't know how to do your maths exercises? Let me teach you. Don't stand outside the window. Just tell me what the sum is. Right, now go and get a notepad and a pencil. And so the seventeen-year-old girl did not jump down from the window.

Yet another telephone line goes like this: Is it Auntie A / Auntie B / Auntie C / Cousin D? Do come to the wedding banquet on Sunday. It starts at eight. And so Aunties A, B, C and Cousin D all say:

— Send a bright red invitation card first

And yet another telephone line goes like this: My most Undear Boss, I don't like working for you anymore, and I don't want to see you again. Your most Disobedient Servant hereby gives notice of resignation by telephone. And so the Boss's secretary says:

— We would appreciate it if you could put that in writing

The hotline says: Please press the button. Please press the button. And so we don't know what eventually happens to the hotline.

Chief Inspector

Of course I am continuing with my chart; I have also added further details to the telephone handset. This time I have drawn an ear. My view of the ear and the telephone is like this: whoever invented the ear had forgotten about an ear-cap. You see, the mouth has lips, so it can decide not to talk or eat. The eyes have eyelids, so they can decide not to see. But the poor ear cannot be zipped up; it has to listen to all sorts of noise pollution. Whoever invented the telephone has also forgotten to make an ear-cap for it, and so it allows noise to charge through the thickest walls and the tightest doors and windows and scream in any room. However, there are some who see it different: television sets emit radiation and are harmful to the eyes; telephone sets are not harmful to the ear.

Senior Technicians
Technicians
Technical Trainees

The engineer has just mentioned technical trainees. He says: it's not a bad thing to join this company as a technical trainee really. You get the chance to do field work every year, and you can come here to attend classes. He says that this room where you are sitting is a classroom, that this is where the lessons will be taught, that it is their own training school. And then he suddenly asks us:

— do any of you live very far from here

— those who do please raise their hands

Over half of the people have their hands up. As for me, of course I live far away. This is Lily Pond, and I live in the City Centre. I had to get up at six this morning.

I spent half an hour queuing for the bus, and another forty-five minutes hanging onto a steel pole inside the bus. I figure that forty-five minutes in the bus is a long journey, thus I put my hand up, too.

The many hands that are put up in the classroom are like Chinese cabbages sprouting suddenly in a field. Thus the engineer takes out of a thick paper bag a number of coins of a low denomination, and all those who have raised their hands get six coins.

— this is a special travel allowance

— of course we're not inviting you to come by cab

he says. The fact is, several people did come by cab. The engineer also says that we will all need to eat when we work for the telephone company, and since we will be eating during our work hours, that concerns the company. Since that is the case, the company will pay for our meals. However, it is quite a lot of trouble handing out meal money every day, so it will be incorporated into our monthly salaries. And the same will hold for any other allowances and bonus payments. When he gets to this point, his words have made everyone hungry. The fact is, all our watches have raised the number 1.

— let's break for lunch

— the cafeteria is on the third floor

the engineer says. And so everyone bids him a happy, temporary farewell.

Now I'm inviting myself to lunch. I see written on one board French Toast Ovaltine and suchlike; on another board it is Garoupa in Cream Corn Sauce with Rice Singaporean Noodles Minced Beef with Rice and suchlike. Everyone is standing in front of a long counter giving their order and making payment, so I do the same.

The cafeteria where I'm having my meal is, naturally, part of the telephone company's training school. Right now there are many people in the cafeteria. Some of them were sitting with me in the classroom, which means the others must be attending classes in the school. They sit together in threes and fours, together with their cardboard files. The files are stuffed with paper, some of which are sticking out, and so the corners are dog-eared.

There are several young men sitting round a table. One of them opens his file and reads as he eats. The papers in the file include some pencil-drawn charts as well as typewritten lecture notes handed out by the teacher.

— I wonder if this one will come up in the exam

says a young man munching on a piece of garoupa. He is so thorough about munching the piece of fish that you'd think the fish would come up in the exam.

— oh I wish the teacher would tip us off

says another young man. On hearing this, a few people sitting in a corner near them smile; they are all teachers at this school. On hearing this, the man standing behind the counter busy serving food also smiles, saying:

— who else is for tipping

— who else

However, no one seems to show any interest in what he says, so he has no choice but to hurry off to fetch a few glasses of tea.[3]

The person sitting across from me has gone to stand in front of the counter. When he gets his tea, he comes back to our table. Just a while

---

[3] Tea is served in glasses in cafeterias and cheaper restaurants in Hong Kong.

ago we were in the classroom together. Just a while ago, we didn't know each other. But now, we have nodded to each other, and we have spoken to each other. So it seems that to progress suddenly from complete strangers to partners in conversation is really no big deal. A while ago we were sitting across a table.

— are you new too

he asked.

— yes I'm new too

I replied. And that was it. After that, we no longer had to focus our eyes on our own plates, and we no longer had to bury our heads in the plate to do a rice-count. And now, as he comes back from the counter, he has two glasses of tea in his hands, and he gives one to me. As I drink the tea, a thought occurs to me: Yes, why else did people invent the telephone? Wasn't it because they wanted to talk to each other?

It is said that the public phone was made available to us humans in the year 1877. Who knows what things will be like by the year 2877; perhaps we'd be able to hold a soundless conversation through thought-telepathy. By that time, will the telephone have become what letters are to us now? We are too lazy to pick up our pens now, and we will be too lazy to pick up the phone by then.

Some people actually turn silent after they acquire a telephone. There is this man who just happened to dial a wrong number, and the voice at the other end said: Mortuary.[4] Some people say that when you're in a theatre, and all of a sudden the phone rings urgently on stage with no one there to take the call, the sense of fear you experience is particularly strong.

And now I have returned to the classroom. The atmosphere in here has obviously changed. Everyone who was quiet before is now talking in twos and threes. For instance, I myself am talking to the chap who just

---

[4]This is a reference to the practice of some irritable people who try to get back at people who have dialled the wrong number. Since death is normally a taboo among older Chinese, the idea of having called up the mortuary can be upsetting to certain people.

gave me some tea. He says that he has come to work as an office boy after having been unemployed for three months.

This time round the engineer shows us some slides about the goings-on in various departments in the company. As the lights are dim in the room, I no longer draw charts on pieces of paper. I just try to make a mental note of all that I can remember. Actually, there are some departments which I just forget as soon as they have been mentioned, like the general affairs department, the warehouse department, the marketing department, the estate department, the workshop department, the transport department, and the civil engineering department.

The department I remember most clearly is the international telephone services department. It turns out that this department is called 100, and it specializes in connecting local citizens to long-distance calls. I also remember the outdoors works department. Now I recall that I've come across people working in this department many times before, only I've never paid much attention to them. They are the people who rope off a section of the street, then either dig a hole in the middle or lift off a round cover in the ground, and then squeeze themselves inside to work underground. They go under the street to lay the telephone wires.

The engineer says besides telephone wires, there are various lines and pipes such as electricity cables, gas pipes, and water pipes. And when I was walking down the street I always thought there was nothing but my shoes and asphalt underfoot.

It suddenly occurs to me: when I was at school, though the people who stood in front of the blackboard were not inclined to smile, what they said always made a lot of sense. For instance: Look up at the sky; how much do you know about the sky? Now look down at the earth, how much do you know about the earth?

The engineer says that there is also an underground railway design department in the telephone company. This department I finally manage to remember. And I also remember the installation department which instals new telephones for customers. As for others such as the phone line interchange design department, or the Strowger exchange repairs department, well, my brain stretches two hands out to shove them away.

When the engineer mentions the customer services department I know I have found what I am looking for. Right, customer services, here I come, I say. And so I pay special attention to all that's said. The engineer says: this department is responsible for telephone repair jobs in customers' homes. Anyone in the city can dial 109 when their telephones go wrong, and we immediately take down their number and send someone to attend to the repair. At the moment, says the engineer, the customer maintenance department is also responsible for laying some overground telephone wires, but in the future such work will be taken over by the installation department.

As the engineer gets to this point, my brain suddenly tells me:

— I'm tired

Naturally my brain only talks to me. The strange thing is, it seems to have given the engineer a call as well, for he actually knows about it. He immediately changes the subject and talks about fringe benefits and the like.

— public holidays are of course days off

— if you work on those days, you get double pay

he says. As for the departments offering round the clock service, days off will be arranged by the different teams within the department.

— and when you're unwell, there's the company doctor

— seeing the company doctor is of course free

he says. Everyone is entitled to twelve days of sick leave per year. Then he goes on to maternity leave for the women employees. As my brain is tired, I shut it down. However, I have not missed the engineer's last few words:

— goodbye everyone

— hope you'll enjoy your work

I've come to work for them, and the place I report to is the city centre exchange. In the exchange I am greeted by a supervisor. When he learns that I'm fresh from school, he gives me some words of encouragement which last a minute long, and tells me to work hard, etc. I answer that I will, whereupon he sends me to the maintenance department to go out with others to change telephone wires.

At this moment, a chap whose hair is as long as mine, and who wears jeans like mine, and whose skin is the colour of sunshine, like mine, comes up to me.

— I'm Merry Mak

he says. He also says: though a big bunch of us go out to change telephone wires, we work in pairs. As from today, we're partners, so we should look after each other.

— I'm Fruits

I say. Seeing that he has long hair like mine, and wears jeans like mine really makes me happy.

First thing, he takes me into a storeroom and gets a pile of things for me. Then he gets hold of a dark green canvas bag with four white letters on it — acronym for the company. Then he gets hold of pliers, big hammers, small hammers and over a thousand brass studs. Then he puts all the hammers and nails and what not into the bag, hands it to me, and says: It's yours.

We come out of the exchange into the street. As I swing the canvas bag onto my back, it feels like I'm going to Big Wave Bay for a picnic; it also feels like the old days when I went to school. In those days, of course, my canvas bag was filled with history and geography. In those days, of course, I had to wear a school uniform.

Today we are going to continue the job of changing a set of telephone wires in this street. This job has already gone on for several months, it being a big project. We are stationed in pairs under the balconies, at a distance of ten to twenty paces apart. To me, we're just like a squad of soldiers.

The balconies in the street are the old style sheltered walkway. This is an old street. At this moment, loops and loops of disconnected telephone wires are hanging on the wall along the walkway. They form a pattern of waving curves, just like festival lights in the streets.

I stride alongside Merry Mak.

— d'you like swimming

— d'you like climbing hills

he asks me. He says he likes fishing, and hiking, and watching football, and if I'm interested, we can go rowing together some time. Of course I like swimming and rowing, so I tell him that next time he'll have to count me in. He then asks me whether I like chilies. At this I shake my head. He then says: chilies are good things.

We've come to the foot of a staircase. He throws his bag on the ground, takes a sheet of newspaper from his jeans pocket which is marked with a big letter, tears the newspaper into two halves, gives me one half, and keeps the other for himself. I get it. He's obviously fond of films and wants to invite me to one. That's why he gives me the newspaper to see if there are any good films. So I start looking at the paper, and after a bit of searching, I tell him that perhaps we can go and see Clint Eastwood.

It turns out that Merry Mak is also fond of Clint Eastwood films. However, he says, we have some handicraft to do first. He then tells me to spread the newspaper on the ground and follow him step by step. I do as he says, and find that I've made myself a hat. We put our hats on. I say: now we can have a masquerade.

He laughs out loud and goes to the staircase hallwell to bring out a wooden ladder, which he sets against the wall. He then asks me to watch over it as he climbs. When he gets to the top of the ladder, he pulls out some brass studs from the wall and undoes the old telephone wire. After loosening the line, he hangs it carefully on another stud.

I stand under the ladder, looking up at him to see how the work's done. Pounds of dust from the telephone wires fall down, so I quickly rub my eyes.

— don't look up

— I'll tell you how to do it later

he shouts from above. And so I revert my head to normal horizontal position. For a good while I keep staring at the ladder. Well, he told me to watch the ladder so that pedestrians won't knock it and cause him to

fall down, and I am doing just that. After a while, since I have nothing
much to do, and there's so much going on in the street, my eyes shift from
the ladder to other places.

The young man who just walked by — he's got curly hair.[5]

And the young fellers on this side — they've all got beards.

And there are *so* many people in jeans.

Sandals are *such* comfortable things.

All these cork platform shoes the girls are wearing make them look
like princesses in the Qing court.

So, the shop over there is a general store. A thin shopkeeper is
standing outside, using a forked pole to hang up string after string of goods
outside the shop front. Soon all sorts of goods are hanging from that rack:
bamboo baskets, plastic baskets, kettles, scrubbing boards. And a while
later, it looks like the whole shop is hanging from the rack. All the shops
in this street have goods hanging outside their shop fronts. When people
walk past, they seem to have walked into a forest of manufactured
products, with all sorts of strange foliage growing overhead.

— let's take a break

— what about a soft drink

All of a sudden Merry Mak is standing in front of me. Only now do
I recall that I'm standing under the ladder. He hands me an icy cold bottle
of soft drink the colour of black dates. He lifts the bottle to his lips and
gulps down the drink, while I keep sucking at a paper straw.

After we finish the drink, Merry Mak says: Your turn now. He tells
me that all I have to do is pull the telephone wire off; it's up to me how
to do it. He also tells me that there are other kinds of lines up there, and
I have to make sure I don't make a mistake: the telephone wire is grey,
thin and round, and there are two lines stuck together, while the electricity
cable is thicker and black, and there's only one of it.

---

[5] The majority of Chinese people have straight black or dark brown hair, but starting
from the early 1970s it became trendy for young men in Hong Kong to perm their hair for
a more stylish look.

As I climb the ladder, the instructions are: No need to be afraid. Though there is live electricity in the wires, it's only fifty volts, so it won't give you an electric shock. In no time I've got to the top, and the first thing I do is to steady myself on the ladder. (I suppose I may have a future as a trapeze artist.) I hold onto the ladder with one hand and pull out the telephone wire with the other. With a pair of long-nosed pliers I pull out the brass studs from the wall. (I suppose I may have a future as a dentist.) And then I hang the wire on one of the studs.

Merry Mak stands under the ladder to keep watch for me. He puts one foot on the ladder and starts talking to me. He says that he did this yesterday: he put a pair of jeans into a bucket of diluted bleach, with the result that the jeans have become old and faded. He goes on to say that since we're out in the streets installing telephone wire, we should dress as shabbily as possible. He looks at the jeans I'm wearing: That's what we want. Coarse clothes suit us best.

After working for a while, I become quite used to it. I no longer need to hang onto the ladder, but can work with both hands. (I suppose I may have a future as a construction worker.) I think I have quite an interesting job, standing so high up above the street, looking at the pedestrians hurrying about their business. Sometimes one or two of them look up at me, and when they do I feel like asking: Don't you think I have an interesting job? And what's your job?

When I was still at school I came across this title for a composition in class: my ambition. At that time I wrote: When I grow up I'll be a postman, and after that I'll be a street sweeper, and after that a fireman, and after that a farmer, and after that a fisherman, and after that a policeman. It just happened that my social studies text book listed all these occupations.

All of a sudden Merry Mak tells me to come down, and so I climb down the ladder. I figure he probably thinks I'm too slow and too clumsy, but what he says is:

— time for lunch
— work can wait

Lifting the ladder on one shoulder and holding onto it with one hand, he takes many steps back to the hallwell, puts the ladder against the wall on the ground floor, wipes his hands on his backside, and comes out. All the teams of two changing telephone wires in this street have put down their work; they have put their pliers and working gloves back into their bags. They take their paper hats off, fold them small, and put them in their back pockets. Those groups at both ends of the street signal to each other, and then start walking in the same direction. And so I too pick up the canvas bag that's now mine, and walk side by side with Merry Mak, following the others.

As is their custom, they walk up to a restaurant and occupy two tables fronting the street. After a few dishes — nothing fancy — have been ordered, they start eating and drinking. I follow them in some of the things they do, like drinking strong *puer* tea, finishing two bowls of rice, and using a toothpick to clean my teeth. However, I do not follow them in some other things, like putting my feet on a chair, or studying the animal press.[6]

Almost half of the people sitting around these two tables have their heads buried in the animal press. They fold the paper into a quarter of its size and, pen in hand, circle names in it. By the look of them, you'd think that they're going to sit their final exam in no time.

As for the two men sitting across from me, they are exchanging views on the paper they're reading. One of them points at the back of one paper, saying: This mugger who picks on old folks is a real stinking bastard.

There's this other man who has put his head on the table and fallen asleep. They say that he went straight from work onto a ferry to Majao yesterday. When he got to Majao, he boarded a bandit ship[7] and started the battle at around seven in the evening. The battle did not end until the

---

[6]There are newspapers in Hong Kong which specialize in analyses and forecasts of horse races.

[7]This refers to a floating casino in Macau, one of the most popular gambling spots for Hong Kong people.

next morning, when he hurried off to catch his ferry back. That is why he's so tired that he has fallen asleep over lunch. Merry Mak says the chap sleeping over his lunch goes to Majao about a hundred times a year, but should anyone ask him whether Sao Paulo is a beautiful building,[8] he would have said: Sao Paulo, what's that? Never seen it. And if the person should then say that Sao Paulo is the name of a church, that it's the Church of Sao Paulo, and that what's left of this church now is just its front door which looks like a monument, and that people don't call it the Sao Paulo anymore, instead they call it Show Parlour. At this the man who is sleeping over his lunch would have said: Show Parlour? What's that? I've never played that game before. Is it like show hand?

The man who is sleeping over his lunch is soon woken up, for it is now stretch-and-yawn time. Everyone takes out three coins, and these are collected for paying the bill. As they walk down the stairs, the animal press lot are still clutching their pens.

Merry Mak and me return to where we were working, and he goes to get the ladder out on his own and climbs up again. As he is climbing the ladder, I notice that on his beige suede shoes there are hand-painted stars, clouds and rainbows.

— I painted these myself
— what d'you think of them

I think the shoes look interesting. Merry Mak says that though he paints pictures on shoes, it doesn't mean that he wants to become an artist. It's just that there are some stains on the shoes which cannot be washed off, and since he couldn't put shoe polish on suede, he drew stars and clouds on them instead. And now I notice that the cuffs of his jeans are trimmed with wide piping. He says it's all because the jeans have shrunk after washing, so he had to lengthen them with this piece of cotton cloth.

All afternoon Merry Mak and me take turns to do the work, but he always takes the longer shift. Though my head and face are completely

---

[8] The best known building in Macau, this sixteenth century Catholic cathedral was destroyed in a fire. All that remains of it is the facade, which is a landmark in Macau.

covered in dust, I feel very good. By the time we take the ladder back to the hallwell, it's already 5 p.m. Merry Mak tells me that we won't have to go back to the telephone exchange, and tomorrow we won't have to report for duty either. We'll just come straight to this street to work. He also tells me to take the canvas bag home with me because, for the time being, it's mine.

All our mates working in this street have gone. Loops and loops of telephone wires are hanging under the balconies, some hanging all the way to the ground, forming a pile of circles. After locating a public phone booth at a corner of the street, Merry Mak and me step inside, for we have to call the exchange to tell them that we've knocked off. I watch as he lifts the handset and lightly presses one side of the phone, and after a while, he presses again. He has not inserted the three necessary coins; he has just pressed the phone several times, and he actually gets through. As a result I keep staring at his hand, can't take my eyes off it. After he puts down the handset, he gives me a matey pat on the shoulder.

— it's very simple

— you'll be able to do it in a few days

The few days have gone by, and now I'm really able to do it. I've learned a lot of other things as well. For instance, I've got to know about walls. Since I have to hammer studs into the walls, of course I've got to know them. Some walls are soft, and when I hammer a nail in, they cry: here comes a cigarette, hurry up everyone. Since they like cigarettes, they clutch the nails in their mouths. Some walls are hard, and they look fierce, so at the mere sight of them, nails feel afraid and bend their knees. The fiercest of them all are the concrete walls. They don't like making friends with nails. This kind of uncooperative attitude on the part of concrete walls has caused some people to come up with different methods aimed at breaking them down, to make them less reserved, more understanding. And so a type of nail for concrete walls came into being. But one day, something like this happened: as an engineer was trying to blast a nail into a concrete wall with a nail-gun, the wall flung a hand out to shoot the nail back. That rebounding nail found its way into the engineer's heart, and the force knocked him down. This insistence on the part of the concrete wall to keep itself to itself has caused many people to shake their heads and sigh.

Whenever I have to hammer a brass stud into the wall, I always test the attitude of the wall first. In the street where I work, the walls are all very friendly. All I have to do is put a small nail in the eye of the stud and hammer at it lightly, and the nail sinks into the wall. Sometimes, if the nail is too long, I shorten it. And sometimes the wall may reject a nail for no obvious reason, so I use a nail for concrete walls as a scout. After sharpening it, I make a small hole in the wall with it before hammering in the real nail.

To begin with of course I was not very good at the job. The hammer often hit my fingers instead of the nails. And so when I went home in the evenings, my mother Grace would ask: My son, what's the matter with your hands? And I replied: My hands are trying to grow carrots. After a while, my hands no longer grew carrots. I can now hammer away at hundreds of nails a day, and none of them bends.

— there's no secret to hammering studs
— practice makes perfect

says Merry Mak, and he's right again. I've also learned to while away many happy hours every day in the streets. Most of the time I'm standing on top of the ladder, looking up as I work. Since I'm always looking up, I see the sky all the time, and so this thought occurs to me: wouldn't it be nice if this wooden ladder is a ladder to heaven. If that's the case I can climb up and up, all the way up to where old man heaven lives, and there I'd be sure to see the giant, and the giant's hen that lays golden eggs. Why, I can take that hen down with me and give it to the children's library at the City Hall.

9

They say: The railway station will soon move to this place. The man, upon hearing this, takes out his pocket calculator. I'll have to raise the price of my flat by thirty thousand, he says. Last time, because someone said that the Cross Harbour Tunnel on this side of the harbour would come out somewhere near here, this man raised the price of his flat by twenty thousand. That flat of his is still sitting here, empty.

Across from the empty flat, there is a fairly sizable car showroom where there are six or seven new cars in the display windows all the year round. Once, however, what was on display was an antique car, and anyone who sat inside it looked as though they were sitting in a bridal sedan chair. Underneath the showroom building there is a tunnel-type road linking the streets on either side, and sometimes pedestrians make use of this road. Cars waiting for repair are parked along both sides of this road, and often car-enthusiasts would spend a few minutes on each car, giving their individual car reviews: This one isn't much good for climbing slopes; that one is a petrol guzzler.

This is an interesting place for a car showroom. The front of the showroom looks perfectly normal, with the display windows and the petrol station, but at the back it's another story. At the south end of its back door is a cul-de-sac where vehicles can come in and park like boats in a bay. The other end of the cul-de-sac — the only entrance for the cars — is the dead centre of

the food market.

Every morning at eight-thirty, the food market starts its rapid expansion. Besides the usual general stores, fish stalls and barbecue meat stalls, there are racks of bean curd and buckets of bean sprouts on the pavements. By the side of the racks and buckets there'd be a huge tray of eggs, as well as baskets of chickens and ducks. Occasionally you'd see a hutch of rabbits. And occasionally a coop of grey pigeons.

Next to the pavement gutters is a row of vegetable stands, and in the middle of the stands is a cart covered in flowers. The middle of the road features mobile pedlars and their huge bamboo baskets, some of them selling straw mats and towels, others colourful clay dolls and porcelain bowls, yet others lace and ribbons.

Every morning, a large number of people come to the food market with their shopping baskets or string bags or empty hands. They walk on the pavements; they walk in the middle of the road. At such times a car always comes driving in, tooting its horn. It's obvious that this car has just come from another city — brown paper is still stuck all over its body. Looks like a partly opened postal parcel. The car, on which hangs a temporary number plate, drives in carefully.

As the car comes into the food market, it cries *blare, blare* all the way. And so the vegetable stalls and the fish stalls tug and pull and retreat a little from the middle of the road; the white rabbits and the grey pigeons squeeze and push and duck and finally clear a slit of a road. There's sure to be a couple of stalls rowing over this every time. A head sticks out of the window of the incoming car, looking carefully at the car's tail, and then the car moves ahead inch by inch.

Sometimes the vehicle that comes in is a truck on which pigs may be hanging upside down, their ears absolutely immobile. Or there may be fish swimming in the truck. Sometimes the fish would jump down from the truck to the ground. The water in the fish truck seems to think that watering the street is its responsibility, so even on sunny days in the dry season, the street in the food market is forever sopping wet, playing mirror to the buildings nearby.

And when the vehicle has gone, the mobile stalls start pushing and squeezing again. These reassembled stalls grow in size with every reformation. Finally, there isn't even space in the whole street for one person to squeeze past.

Liberty comes to this market behind the showroom to do her shopping, and she always brings her shopping basket with her. She buys eggs every time, and occasionally she also buys a slim bouquet of flowers.

There is this customer at the vegetable stand who picks up one leafy vegetable, presses it, then picks up another one in her other hand and presses it, making a comparison. The result is that she puts both back and presses yet another one. In this way she manages to turn almost all the vegetables upside down.

Liberty is fond of the plump and squat white-stem vegetable. They look just like light-bulbs. One time Liberty bought some, and when she got home she arranged them in a soup bowl and displayed them on the dining table. She admired them for a whole morning before cooking them for lunch. Every time Liberty buys vegetables, she says: One catty please. The woman pedlar lines up the vegetables very neatly in three rows, and then ties them up with raffia string. She also gives Liberty some free spring onions. Liberty keeps the spring onions for planting on the rooftop of No. 1 Hobby Horse Road, and so there is now a whole wood-chestful of spring onions on the rooftop, like rice seedlings.

Whenever Liberty needs to go into the city centre, she walks to the bus stop in front of the showroom. This is a very strange bus stop whose moods are impossible to forecast. Sometimes the people waiting for the buses form a nice, orderly queue despite the fact that there is no stationmaster here. And sometimes they just occupy strategic positions and, as soon as the bus comes in, jostle each other, fighting to get on.

Many vehicles pass this bus stop. There are the fourteen-seat minibuses; there are the buses that go to the various piers; there are the taxis hired by groups of five strangers who are now sitting together inside, and there are various tunnel buses. Liberty once met a bus whose door flattened her shoe. However, she also met a tunnel bus which stopped for her when she waved from afar, waited for her as she came running down the long road, and waited till she boarded. The thing about buses is that their moods are also pretty unpredictable.

While they wait for the bus, people standing at the bus stop always look at the things around them, and they always look at the small park across from the bus stop. There are no trees and no flowers in the park, but there is a pavilion on the side next to the road, and benches and swings, and on the other side there is a sports field.

Liberty often sees a teacher in sports gear taking his students to this sports field in the park; she doesn't know which school they're from. The people at the bus stop turn to look for a while at the students doing their exercises, and then turn around to check for remote signs of buses coming from afar.

Near the bus stop there are a few park benches. Liberty remembers that these benches were once home to a tramp. At seven in the morning, when everyone was waiting for the bus, he was still asleep, a great black lump lying on the park bench. At one end of the bench there was also a bundle of things Liberty couldn't make out.

In the afternoons, people waiting for the bus could see the tramp squatting on the ground alone. In front of him there were a stove, a frying pan, a mug for rinsing his mouth, and a small tin. He was carefully cooking the vegetable leaves and rotten carrots which he had picked up in the market. He was also smoking. His hair was matted, hard as an iron board. Children surrounded him, but he seemed oblivious to the world around him. He gave all his attention to his culinary creation.

However, it was not long before the tramp declined to show his face, and the people queuing for buses no longer remember him. His is of course not a traditional drama. Since there had been no prelude, there was no reason why he should have performed till the curtain fell.

Liberty likes to take a walk, as long as she has the time. The fact is, there isn't much she can do if she stays home. The people at home are all caught up in playing mahjongg; it's much better to stroll down the main street. When Liberty gets out of the house, she always comes to this road lined with oleanders. She sees, and notices, the many changes that have taken place.

Do you remember your primary school days? What was your school like? When Liberty comes to the slope where oleanders grow, she looks to see whether her school is still there, whether the students still plant any flowers.

Liberty's primary school was a tiny school. There was just one big hall. Half of it was the classroom, the other half was where people came in to rest and chat: it was the common room of the railway workers. On Saturday evenings they even had film shows here. Everyone who worked for the railway, or even those who were just passing by, could go in and watch.

On weekdays, half of this hall served as a classroom. Four classes of students sat there, from Year One to Year Four. They all sat there in the big room, and when one class was having a lesson, the others quietly did their school exercises. When it was time for the next class to have their lesson, the first class started to work on their drawings.

Liberty remembers that the blackboard was movable, not nailed to the wall. Instead it was like a painting in progress, resting on an easel.

Liberty was particularly fond of music lessons. They had a special music room — a train carriage. This carriage was stationed on a track quite close to the school hall, and it was a real train carriage. There was a piano inside, and when everyone took their seat in the carriage for class, it was like going on a long trip. As they sang they gave free rein to their imagination: Surely we'll see a beautiful lake at the next station.

As Liberty walks past the slope of oleanders, she sees that the train carriage is still there. It had travelled to faraway places in the hearts of so many, and now it's back, there to stay. There is a railway tunnel next to the carriage, and trains bound for the New Territories still blow their whistles as they go through it. On the other side of the tunnel there used to be railway corporation quarters, but that has all gone. In their place are a new garden and criss-crossing flyovers.

As Liberty walks past the slope with oleanders, she sees that the small house with a round roof is still there — a military-camp style house. Its roof is round, with a pattern like that of corrugated paper, its walls are whitewashed, and there are windows on two sides. The middle part of this house used to be the headmaster's quarters, and on either side were the classrooms for Year Five and Year Six. There is an expanse of ground outside the house with some railway tracks running on it, and a few train carriages are scattered along these tracks.

When Liberty sat in the classrooms in the house with a round roof, she could see the scenes outside the windows. She often saw several people unloading a sack from a train, and in the sack there were human bones. Because of this, no one ever dared use the desolate toilet at one end of the path there.

When Liberty went to school, she walked past the Final Farewell Pavilion every day. She had seen many many people cry, people who all wore white. There was someone who said their final farewell almost every day. A few grey train carriages would be stationed across from the entrance to Final Farewell Pavilion; sometimes there would be a sign hanging on the carriage door, sometimes not. There was just one letter on the plaque: Y. This was like plates of the same shape which have only one letter on them: L. When an L is hanging from a vehicle, that means the person inside is learning to drive. When a Y was hanging on a carriage door, it meant that there was a coffin inside which would soon be taken by train to the countryside.

People who walked past here were used to seeing the letter Y on the train carriages, so no one was scared by it. As for the casual passers-by, they might not even have an idea of what Y meant. Since this road was wide and flat, there were always a few kids staying behind after school to ride their bicycles.

The grounds next to the house with a round roof were empty, and the teacher said: Why don't we grow some vegetables here. And so he brought some seeds and tools, and everyone lent a helping hand. Soon the empty grounds turned into a fertile field. After school, everyone went to water the vegetables, and those who weren't afraid of worms tried to catch worms. They had mustard plants which were thin, each looking like a ruler, but they also had white-stem vegetables that were fat, each looking like a globe.

Pumpkins grew one by one on the ground, while potatoes all hid underground. In the sweet pea flowering season, there were tiny blossoms in the fields. Bamboo sticks had to be stuck into the sweet pea beds because the sweet pea grows tendrils. When the sweet corn began to bear fruit, everyone wrapped the cobs in paper bags. And so the sparrows that passed by said:

— no fruits in the field

— let's eat the pastry crumbs on the ground instead

Liberty went to school twice a day. Many times at noon she would walk to school behind a funeral procession, watching as she went. In the street she saw the coffin being taken down a bamboo ramp leading from a balcony to the street.[1] All those concerned would cry and moan, and the funeral band would play its brass instruments, making a sort of western music which did not really sound sad.

At noon, when Liberty went back to school after lunch, she would often come across a funeral procession in the street. At this point the wharf hooter sounded, and hundreds of people came out of a dozen tiny doors of the wharf. Most of them were in overalls stained with old and new paint, and the road looked like a beach in summer.

As the wharf emitted the hundreds of people, the funeral procession in the middle of the road that was moving slowly forward suddenly gained in numbers. The sound of the wharf hooter blended into the music of the funeral band. And then the funeral procession gradually lost its head, and then its trunk, and then its tail. All the painters carpenters welders electricians from the wharf were scattered along the road, each holding a

---

[1] It was believed that the body of the dead should not use the staircase frequented by the living. A special "exit" had to be constructed for the specific purpose of removing the coffin from the flat. This practice had almost completely disappeared by the early 1980s.

bowl of steaming rice. There were never enough seats at the food stalls, so they just squatted with their backs against the wall, like so many frogs. When people who were hurrying home for lunch saw these men shovelling rice into their mouths, their footsteps quickened.

Soon after the funeral procession had left, another procession came into view from afar. This time it was a joyful event. At the head of the procession were two Taoists in bright red robes embroidered with the *taichi* sign. They had in their hands bells on sticks, like lollipops, which they rang as they walked along: *ding ding ding*. The musicians following in their wake were making festive Chinese music. And then came the people carrying roast pigs on red wooden trays, with flowers stuck on all the pig heads.

Everyone in the oncoming procession was wearing colourful clothes embroidered with gold and silver flowers and decorated with sequins. Over half of them were women, some on foot, some in cars, some holding colourful paper pinwheels, or holding sticks of smoking incense.

In the midst of these people there appeared a huge colourful plaque covered in bows of red satin, and right in the middle there was a round, convex mirror. There were also fresh flowers on the plaque, and pieces of ginger hanging from red strings. These ginger pieces stretched out hands and feet as they swung and dangled. As the plaque moved, they shook and shook, as if nodding their heads saying it's fun it's fun, or was it shaking their heads saying I'm tired I'm tired. The big group of people came from the Guanyin Temple, and walked towards the Earth God's Temple at the other end of the road.

As Liberty walks down the road from the wharf along her old path to school, she does not hear the sound of the hooter. It isn't noon now. She walks down a stone staircase and goes slowly to the bottom of the slope where the oleanders grow. The pavilion in which people often sat crying is now empty. Across from it there are still a few grey train carriages.

Liberty stands in front of a train carriage. She sees that it is tightly shut, and there is a sign hanging on the door. What does the carriage hold now? Liberty sees inside it an open drain, she also sees a street, and a mountain that has been moved to fill the sea.

At this very moment, an ancient post office is being lowered by a huge crane into the carriage. And then a black, noisy train covered in soot runs into the carriage.

Liberty also sees the railway terminal, the clock tower, the grass by the railway line, all inside the train carriage. There are even other grey train carriages inside it, all with a sign on their doors, all saying: Y.

Every day, in this city there are always some things or other quietly bidding us farewell, and then gradually disappearing.

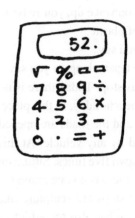

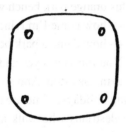

10

When you wake up, you're lying on a postal parcel. The parcel is wrapped in a huge sheet of plastic. This plastic is transparent, so you can see that what is inside is a park bench. What is more, you can also see that the park bench is orange in colour. When you wake up, you're lying on this orange park bench wrapped in a sheet of plastic.

— how come I'm lying on a park bench, you say

— how come a park bench has turned into a parcel, again you say

You rub your eyes and sit up. This is a bus stop. Today there is no one at the bus stop. And so you think: It must be a holiday. In this place, during holidays, some areas are cordoned off, and the roads are opened to pedestrians who walk around, unthreatened by any vehicle. At this thought you stretch yourself three times, and yawn five times. Sitting on the park bench, you look to your left and right: there is no one around.

There is another bus stop over there. Bus stops are sculpture-like pillars of traffic signs. Now you see that this one has also turned into a postal parcel. Wrapped around it is a sheet of opaque plastic, and on top of the plastic there are strings tied tightly into a knot. Perhaps this bus stop will be sent to some exhibition somewhere, you think.

And now you are walking along at your usual pace, and before long you come across an ice-cream van, also wrapped in plastic. You stretch out your hand to get an ice-cream, to no avail. You try your best to untie the knot, to no avail. It is a very unusual

knot, not like any other you have seen before. You try tearing it off, without any success either, for it is not your ordinary plastic. You look at the whole van filled with ice-cream, and there is nothing you can do to get it.

Turning park benches, bus stops and ice-cream vans into postal parcels: some big city somewhere is probably going to hold a Road Show, you think. In that case, other things should be sent there too, like: tunnels, zebra-crossings, traffic lights, police stands. And it's just as you think, for as you walk along, soon you see that the traffic lights, the zebra-crossing, the police stand, and a tunnel, have all been wrapped up.

You would like to ask a passer-by which city is going to host a city scene exhibition, but there is no one around. There is no one in the streets today. You decide to get a newspaper and read about it. When you get to the news-stand, you see that the stand and the paper boy have turned into parcels. Ah, yes, the news-stand will be sent to the exhibition, too, you say. You decide to call up a Citizens' Officer to find out the answer. When you get to the phone booth, you find that even the telephone has turned into a parcel.

Such a strange exhibition, you think, perhaps the whole city will be sent to be exhibited. And so you go everywhere to see what else has turned into parcels. You find that everything has been wrapped up and tied up. The plastic wrapping is transparent, so you can distinguish every object by its shape. From a distance they all look grey, and at closer quarters they seem to have been rinsed in running water.

The usual sights, such as high-rise buildings, the airport, the runway, the ferry pier, have now all been carefully wrapped up; some have become part of a huge parcel, while others have been sorted and are standing there independent parcels. It seems that one man, a very special tailor, has fitted out all objects in the city in tailor-made clothing.

You walk down the road, and it is still recognizable to you because theoretically it has not changed. The difference is just that you feel you have been plunged into a very foggy morning. You come in front of a high-rise building, and just like the rest, it has turned into a parcel. This

is where you come to work every day, and you have long become tired
of it. Seeing that it is now a parcel, an object which has a certain distance
from you, you actually feel quite glad. You think of that desk in the
building, and the typewriter next to the desk, and the documents in the
drawers, and all the faces in the room — just one night's sleep, and you
have shaken them off completely, what a great surprise!

And so you begin to walk home. You walk for a long time, for many
hours. Normally you would have travelled by motor vehicle, but today
there are very few vehicles on the road, and those that you see have all
been wrapped up. You arrive at the place where you live, and in front of
you is a huge plastic sheet. You see that the window you know so well is
behind the plastic, like numerous other windows behind the pale greyish
screen, it looks like a weary eye. You stand there looking a moment, and
then say: Oh, I suppose I can hit the road then. You have always wanted
to hit the road on your own.

Now you are walking towards the countryside. Along the way you
are the only moving object; everything else is stationary, even the wind.
You come across some empty plastic bags floating in the air, with nothing
inside, and you are sure that what is wrapped inside is the wind. There
are also other floating plastic bags and you can see clouds inside them.

You walk past a wall; even the shadow of the wall is covered in a
plastic sheet and tied up like a huge blot of black ink. You walk over the
ink. You keep walking for a long time. You come across a lake and the
squat houses by the lakeside. On the lake there are two embankments
where weeping willows grow. On one shore there is a stall displaying
rustic baskets, all delicately hand-woven. By the side of the stall sits a
man. The lake, the embankments, the stall with its little baskets, and the
squat houses by the lakeside have all fallen into a parcel. You want to
have a look at a basket, but when you stretch your hand out all you feel
is the sticky sensation of non-breathing plastic.

— good morning

you say to the man sitting by the stall. You have not said anything
since early this morning. However, the man sitting by the stall obviously

does not hear you; he just sits there. It seems that the words "good morning" have been wrapped up as soon as they come out of your mouth.

As you walk away from this parcel of a lake, you feel like having a chat with the friends you talk to every day, but you know that there is no chance of finding them. Like your home, and your work place, they would not be the same as yesterday.

You sit down by the roadside and begin singing to yourself for a while. After that you feel that your surroundings really are deserted. You stand up, run about on the road, and roll around on the ground, and then sit down again. Is this all? Is there nothing else? you ask yourself. Suddenly you remember that the desk in the high-rise building has a very tight drawer. Every time you open it, you almost drag the whole desk forward. I'll have to fix that drawer, you tell yourself.

Then you remember that there are two pieces of ham in the fridge at home; the ham goes with bread as part of your breakfast every day. You'd like some bread now, and a cup of coffee. It'd be still better if you could have a cigarette. But everything you see wherever you go is like a parcel waiting to be posted.

And now your thoughts turn to the parcels. It is true that everything is under wraps, but that does not necessarily mean that everything will be sent abroad for exhibition.

Perhaps the wrapping is meant to stop pollution.

Perhaps recently someone has come up with a method for environmental protection: wrap and tie up everything. In this way, noise pollution and polluted air will not be able to get through. This situation is similar to putting a fish in a cellophane bag when you bring it home. Or perhaps the wrapping means people will not come into contact with each other any more. Whether they are objects or humans, if they are wrapped up in plastic, the distance between them will increase. When each is isolated from all else and becomes a subject of greater independence, the friction between them will proportionally decrease.

This situation is similar to the specially designed cardboard egg trays. The eggs are not broken because they are isolated from one another. Or perhaps the reason for wrapping everything up is: the city is going to move. This city may want to move elsewhere, to have a better living environment. This will give the original city time to recuperate; it will also give the air, water, grass, and earth a chance to regain their vitality. This situation is like the need to leave a field fallow after planting so that it can recuperate and restore itself.

Other possibilities also occur to you, for example: the parcels look like rubbish bags which line both sides of a long corridor. You have always put your rubbish into plastic bags. As your thoughts go in this direction, you suddenly hear some sort of yelling in distance.

Since this morning you have not heard any noise, not even birdsong, not even the sound of motors, not even the slight noise of cups clanging against the table. You hear yelling in the distance; it's someone crying out loud, like he was cutting wood, or hammering at the air.

When it occurs to you that there may be someone in the distance, that it is actually a human being, you stand up and go forward, following the sound. You don't walk, you run.

On the open mud flat in front of you, you find the source of the sound you are longing to find. It is a man brandishing a sword. He stands alone there, cutting and thrusting on all sides as he yells. This man is exercising; sword dance is his favourite exercise, you think.

And so you walk towards him and stand watching at a little distance. You see him thrusting his sword again and again on all sides of him, and he also cuts forcefully at the sky above. And then, his hands drop in exhaustion. He has seen you, but as he is still panting, he cannot talk to you, not until he has caught his breath.

At this moment, you are filled with questions. You're just about to sort out your thoughts and put a question to him when he walks over to you. He hands you two things, one is his sword, the other is a huge sheet of plastic. He says: Take your choice.

You can choose the sheet of plastic, spread it out, walk inside, and wrap it around yourself. You'd then become like all other objects — a parcel.

Or you can choose the sword. Sword in hand, you can cut open all the parcels in the city, you can cut the ropes that have tied up all objects, you can cut the screens that seal off all objects. However, there are many, many parcels, and the ropes and plastic are special, new products; the strangest part is, after you have cut them, they sew themselves back up again in no time. Cutting open parcels will therefore be a job you'd never finish.

The swordsman says that he does not have the ability to cut all the ropes and screens, but he does not want to become a parcel either, so he cuts at the sky every day, hoping that he will tear it somewhere so he can get out.

The swordsman puts the two things down on the ground, walks to one side, sits down, and after a while, lies down.

— I'm tired, he says

He closes his eyes, and soon he is fast asleep.

And now you are no longer considering the question of what a parcel is. The question you are faced with is:

do I become a parcel

or do I cut open other parcels

or do I cut open the sky?

You decide to sit down first. And so you sit down. After that you tell yourself to have some sleep first. And so you lie down and close your eyes. Soon you are fast asleep like the swordsman.

It is such an exciting evening, something that people in the city have never seen before. That's why it should be recorded.

It is early evening, and a wind suddenly blows up from nowhere in the centre of the city. It is a dry wind which keeps blowing for a long time, and moths and insects fall out of the sky. After that, a frog falls out of the sky. This frog, upon landing, springs into the air, turns a somersault, croaks a few times, and then leaps and jumps into the gutter by the road side.

After that, the lightning comes. By 6:30 p.m. standard time, there is lots of lightning, the wind is strong, and thunder rumbles. This being the case, the Royal Observatory hurriedly hoists a spherical red signal.

This is the time for the news programme report. The news broadcaster for Channel Seven sits in front of a world map, telling the latest news.

— oil resources have been exhausted

— reservoirs have dried up

he says. As he is saying this, crowds begin to appear in the city streets. The crowds grow bigger and bigger, as if everyone has come out of his house to take part in a lantern festival; every street looks like a packed train carriage. All these people are holding objects in their hands. A closer look reveals that the objects are axes, hammers and saws. Two men are shouldering a wardrobe. Everyone is looking up at the sky, staring like birds of prey at a few clouds.

Among the clouds in the sky, two suddenly collide like cars in a motor accident: they run towards each other from a distance, bump together in head-on collision, make a loud noise, and throw out a ribbon of lightning. This lightning strip is fond of performing in the sky, so it glides along a zig-zag path before flying speedily towards the earth. The people on the streets cry out together: "Here it comes", and there is a mad rush for the lightning. A man with axe in hand is first to get there. He slashes at the lightning with his axe and cuts off a section. Someone at his side immediately gets hold of a black garment, wraps the lightning in it, and stuffs it into the wardrobe. This group, working rapidly and systematically as a team, soon reaps dozens of lightning sections.

The television news in this city is world famous. It often comes up with special news reels which the whole world wants to buy. The frenzied rush to collect lightning has just started a few minutes ago, and now it is being shown live on the screen. The news broadcaster tells the story in an excited voice, a voice which, like commentaries for football or wrestling matches, attracts many ears:

Now we'll take you to the actual scene for an in-depth look. Ah, you see that did you see that? That's it, hack it, hack it off. That was a marvellous swing of the axe, exactly the way the Old Norsemen would have done it. My dear television viewers, did you see that? These people are now trimming the lightning sections down to the right size so that they can be put into fluorescent lights. If this natural source of electricity is preserved well, it will burn for many seasons. This is truly a rich natural resource. A housewife over there has installed the lightning into her stove. This lightning will cook six months' lunches for her. My dear viewers, the recent exhaustion of oil reserves has resulted in a serious energy crisis. In the future we will lose various means of illumination because of this ...

However, no one is listening to the news broadcaster, for everyone has come out into the streets. Some are standing on the roof flying kites, and the kites lead the lightning directly into drawers in their flats. As for the white shirts, sweaters and handbags in the drawers, they have of course been thrown out onto the floor.

There is a woman standing at her window shaking a garment embroidered with metallic pieces, and in that way she catches a few strips of lightning, too. She locks the lightning into her safe. As for the diamond necklaces and jade bracelets that were originally in the safe, they have been thrown into the narcissus pot to lie with the colourful stones from Rain-petal River.

At this moment a huge group of people jump into the sea because a lot of lightning has fallen into the water. Besides people, there are also yachts, ocean liners, navy ships, ferry boats, hydrofoils, barges, barrels and bath tubs. All these are blocking the seaways. Most of the people have put on deep sea diving equipment to recover the lightning which has fallen to the bottom of the sea.

Some of the ships were setting off on a long sea journey and were originally laden with goods. Now all the goods have been thrown into the sea, and the containers are being used for lightning storage. On top of the high-rise buildings, some people are busy increasing the height of the lightning conductors and connecting them to iron rods and electricity cables. There are even a dozen men who are standing on each other's shoulders to form a human pyramid. The person at the top has raised one arm with one finger pointing upwards, and a needle is tied on to that finger. A lot of lightning is collected this way.

Unfortunately, however, the lightning soon stopped. The wind surges all around, after which the sky darkens twice. Then it starts to rain. It is raining so loudly that you'd think someone has thrown the heavens down to earth. At this point, the people's movements change as rapidly as the weather. Everyone on the streets runs back into their houses, and then they return immediately to the streets, bringing with them another set of objects: bowls, plates, jars, cups, basins, buckets, cooking pots, coffee pots, ice-cube trays, steamers. Seeing this, some people think that there is going to be a kitchenware experimental music show. They ask:

— is this organized jointly with the Urban Council

— is the entrance fee a dollar

And there is this man who says he'll have a look at the programme. The truth is, of course, all these people have brought all these objects out to collect rainwater.

It is only right that the news focus programme on television catches up with the latest. And so when several people take a bath tub up to the top of the building to collect rain water, the whole process is shown on the television screen. The man who is now sitting in front of the world map is a news commentator. It is said that the news broadcaster who had appeared at six-thirty had asked for immediate leave so that he could store up drinking water. At this moment he is busy at home trying to arrange everything related to water collection.

Now the news commentator is talking in an agitated tone of voice, quite unlike his usual self. The following is his analysis of the current situation in the city:

Oh, this is a wise move indeed. Since the reservoirs are depleted and the amount of water in them is dwindling, we are faced with a serious water shortage crisis. It is therefore of paramount importance that every citizen collect drinking water from natural sources. In days past, we have tried our best to save and economize; now is the time to work towards storage.

No one in the city is listening to him; everyone is busy taking containers out into the streets to collect water. After a while the news commentator realizes that no one is listening to him, and this actually makes him happy. He speaks for another two minutes, then he lights a cigarette.

It is raining heavily. Rain heavier than heavy is pouring to the ground, splashing up in forceful spray. Many streets, despite their new design and excellent drainage capacity, are now flooded because of the density of the rain. At this moment, a group of ten people decides to block both ends of a street and seal it up with instant glue. They yell "Heave", and hoist the whole street up to take it home. Another group busies itself with an open drain which has not yet been turned into a carriageway. They turn the drain over, empty it of dirty water, turn it back to its original position, and rinse it out quickly. It is immediately filled up with rain, which they carry home.

A fair number of pedestrian subways in the city and the suburbs, as well as the Undersea Vehicle Tunnel and the Sleeping Lion Tunnel, have vanished almost simultaneously. It goes without saying that they have all been taken away as water storage vessels.

The most orderly project is the one headed by the government itself. Come to think of it, this is really an unprecedented event in this city. The steps taken are as follows:

1. a blueprint is generated by computer
2. a battalion of city guards is called up
3. an explosion is set off to blow a huge hole into the top of a mountain

After the hole has been made, the mountain top immediately turns into a crater lake. Six billion eight hundred million gallons of water are collected in one hour, equal to a tenth of the city's current total water storage level. At the bottom of the mountain there is a reservoir, so when the lake on the mountain top is full, the water automatically flows into the reservoir which is equipped with all the necessary facilities such as catchwaters and water ducts. Following the water ducts, the water flows to the treatment plant in Shabox where, after sedimentation, filtering, and purifying, it turns into drinking water.

Meanwhile, all those who live on top floors have pried open their roofs to let the water fall into their flats. Things such as carpets, mattresses, beach mats, pillows and quilts have been dragged over to stop gaps in the windows, while pianos, lifts, cars and offices are used to block doorways. In this way, whole flats are turned into water tanks. All available space is used for this purpose. Most citizens have filled their toilets with drinking water. The staff of a huge private library takes the whole Imperial collection of classical Chinese writings to the roof and makes four walls, turning it into the most cultured reservoir in the world. In a fortnight's time, art magazines all over the world will fight to put this outstanding design on their covers.

The television news commentator, at the sight of citizens being so positive about collecting water, finds it hard to contain his emotions. He throws down his cigarette butt and says: he has never seen such a spirit of co-operation in any other city, and he is deeply moved by it. He is suddenly filled with new hope for the human race and the world. This is how he expresses his thoughts on tonight's unusual events:

There is no need be too concerned about this world. Did you fear that the oil crisis would drive us to an energy disaster? But just look, we have come through safe and sound. You were scared and horrified by the drying reservoirs, and you thought that from now on we would have to lead a desert-style life, but just look how timely the rain has come.

There is no need to despair of this world. Why do you find it necessary to issue a final verdict declaring that the world lacks the ability to carry on just because of such temporary phenomena as environmental pollution and population explosion? Of course you see the disaster caused by the industrial civilization, and you can predict that robots will take the place of humans on this planet. However, these are but signals sent to us by planet earth to put us on our guard, to remind us in our moments of comfort and leisure not to be overindulgent or overextravagant in spending the earth's resources. Should we not try our best to preserve our beautiful planet?

As he gets to this point, his voice is suddenly gone, for the television station has just drowned.

Such an exciting evening is indeed a rare occasion. The city historian has decided to record it in the yearbook. Moreover, a picture of the book-wall reservoir has been acquired and will soon be sealed in the culture capsule, to be handed down to generations to come.

— public holiday; day off
— if you come to work, you get double pay
says the supervisor. He is holding a sheet of paper. He takes up a pen and draws circles to mark out the names on the paper. The way he does this makes you think that the sheet of paper is one of the animal dailies. He says to everybody: The holiday is here, who's coming to work and who's taking the day off?
— me, I'm taking the day off
I yell.
— me too, I'm not coming in, either
another one of us yells. This other person is Merry Mak. Merry Mak always chooses not to come in during the holidays. Work is work, and play is play, that's what he says. He also says: We have holidays because working every day is both too demanding and too boring, that's why holidays are meant for us to rest and to play. Therefore, we should choose to have the day off.

When a holiday comes round, Merry Mak is truly merry. He gets hold of Silly, and the friends of Silly, and the friends of friends of Silly. In casual clothes and rubber-soled shoes, the whole group heads off for the countryside bright and early. Sometimes they go hiking, sometimes they catch crabs, sometimes they go to the outlying islands. This island city consists of many

islands, so there is always somewhere for Merry Mak to go.

Talking about islands, Merry Mak often shows everyone the photographs he keeps in his pocket. Look, he says, last time we went to this place. It's called Big Weed Island, and there is lots of seaweed floating around the island. We all had congee with mud-skippers in it. The whole bowl of congee was filled with fish — tails and all. In the photo, Merry Mak is eating mud-skipper congee, and there are four fish tails sticking out of the bowl.

There are a dozen young men sitting around Merry Mak, all of them having congee. One of them is Silly. He is holding up a fish skeleton and saying that he'll take it home to make a wood block print.

Silly is fond of hiking, and he brings his camera along every time. The camera is always loaded with a seventy-two exposure roll of film, so whenever something takes his fancy, he clicks the shutter and takes a picture. He never pays any attention to matters such as angle or distance, and sometimes he is even disrespectful of the requirements of lighting, so all his photos are rather impromptu.

Some of Merry Mak's photos are taken by Silly. Take this one for example, taken at Scenic O. In this picture Merry Mak and a group of people are digging at a mountain with their spades. We were helping the holiday camp to open up the mountain, Merry Mak says. Merry Mak and Silly had been to a winter camp where everyone got up at seven in the morning to exercise together. That was winter, that was December when white mist came out of the mouth, when the quilts in the winter camp were more lovely than sheep. Since this is a truly impromptu photo, all the people in it have lost their heads — a great pity.

— what do you want to do

someone once asked Merry Mak

— to travel a bit

Merry Mak said. When other people say they want "to travel a bit", they may mean going to Holland to look at the windmills, or going to Spain to watch bullfights. However, when Merry Mak said he wanted "to travel a bit", he just meant travelling in this little city under our feet.

In this little city there are in fact many places worth travelling to. So many tourists come here every day, and besides, there are all those who are hoping to come. People come here because they want to look at the fishing boats here, and the harbour, and the beaches under the summer sun, and the brilliant lights in the city at night.

And yet *we* just walk down the same few busy streets every day, squeezing ourselves through crowds that hurry by, seeing nothing but pale faces. And so people say: Let's go to Paris! Let's go to Rome! Does this little city hold no attraction for you?

The holiday is here, and this time we'll go camping in a big outlying island. We'll live there for two days. If you like rowing, mountain climbing, lying on the grass star-gazing, or just singing out of tune, you're welcome to come with us. And if you have a knapsack, bring it along, Merry Mak says.

I have a green knapsack. Every time I go hiking, camping or holiday-ing, I take the knapsack out of a drawer. I always open it and turn it inside out to see if roaches have been camping in it or not. And then I stuff all the objects for camping into the knapsack. Sometimes I consider: Should I take one T-shirt or two? Should I take a raincoat with me?

My mother Grace always says: Take your raincoat with you. Who knows what the weather will be like. She also insists that I take two T-shirts so that I'd have another change of clothes. I do as she says. Mother goes on to say her usual piece: Be careful when you climb mountains, don't swim alone in deep water, and don't get into fights. I tell her I'll do as she says. And so I put my green knapsack on my back and go camping with Merry Mak, and his friends, and his friends' friends.

As usual, Mother puts several ten dollar notes into my pocket. This time, however, I shake my head and say that I have money of my own. I can be my own guest when I go camping now.

I do not have a tent, but Merry Mak's friends do. I do not have a sleeping bag, but Merry Mak's friends do. I meet up with Merry Mak at the ferry pier for the outlying islands. He has come early, and is now standing against the railing with a group of friends. On his back is a knapsack that looks like a jellyfish. A water bottle hangs from his shoulder, and he has a stick in one hand and a bag of charcoal in the other. After testing the weight of the charcoal, he puts it back on the ground.

I see Silly, who looks like a sailor in his striped T-shirt. He tells me that he is Silly, and I tell him that I am Fruits, and so we get to know each other. He has a camera in his hands, and is taking pictures of this and that and everything. When we start chatting about things, he asks me how many pots of chilies I have on the rooftop now, whether they're fat or not, whether their colours are bright or not.

There are many people at the pier, all wearing brightly coloured clothes; I see a lot of orange and lemon colours. You won't see these colours at school. In front of the school blackboards, it's always black or white. In the summer it's white; everyone looks like a piece of chalk. In the winter it is dark blue; everyone looks like a blackboard.

A loudspeaker blares at the pier, urging everyone to board the ferry: The express ferry is scheduled to depart at 10 a.m. Please start boarding, please start boarding. Some people start running, others stuff the last piece of rice roll into their mouths. Finally, the ferry blows its horn and bids the pier farewell.

At this moment, on a desert island, someone is standing on the beach. This is a very small island which has neither houses nor inhabitants. Yesterday, a small boat brought this person to this desert island, left him with some drinking water and allowed him a small ration of matches, rice, tinned food, a lunch box, and a spoon and a fork. Then the boat left.

This person is not a prisoner in exile, neither is he being punished. He is here to live on the desert island for three days in the Robinson Crusoe fashion. This is part of a course for the youth leadership camp. The desert island is used to train youth leaders. In the past few days he had been living in camp. Like all the youths in training, he got up at five-thirty in the morning, put on his swimming trunks and sports shoes, and ran ten times round the grounds of their hostel. After that they jogged to the seashore by the pier and immersed themselves in the water. Even in the cold of December, they must immerse themselves in the water.

When they came back from the seashore, they washed and showered, and then cleaned the doors, windows and floor of the hostel. After everything was in order, they assembled on the sports ground to hoist the flag. The device on the flag is a blue compass. The headmaster came to address them every morning. All the youth leaders have to remember to work ceaselessly to improve themselves to be proud and unbending in honest defeat and humble and gentle in victory to overcome all difficulties. After that came breakfast time, with oatmeal, eggs and congee. Everyone was well fed.

Breakfast on the desert island does not feature oatmeal, eggs and congee, unless in a dream. To spend three days all alone on a desert island, the feeling is really strange. There is absolutely no one around. Who can you talk to? You can sing to yourself, or run around on the hills, or swim in the sea, but you cannot talk to anyone.

The person standing on the beach spent the whole of yesterday swimming. His wet clothes dried in no time, and then they became wet again when he went into the water. Except for a raincoat he has no other clothing. He tried to catch clams on the beach, and he looked for twigs to fish with, and he tried to think of all sorts of ways to pass the time. As the sun set and rose, one day passed.

He has no watch, so he does not know the time. He has no idea whether it is now eight in the morning or three in the afternoon. He slept on the beach for a very long time, and when he woke up he thought it must be night. But when he opened his eyes, the sun was shining brightly over his head. He dozed off many times in this way, and whenever he opened his eyes it was still broad daylight.

There is a notebook in his knapsack, so he can keep a diary. He was actually allowed to take some books with him, or paper to draw pictures on, but he did not. He thought that three days would go by very quickly. Swimming, fishing, and sleeping many times — and yet only one day has passed. Now he wishes he had a thick story book with him, but he doesn't. All he has is the small notebook. What to write about? Should he write about his listless leisure, or should it be his determination to bear up no matter how insupportable the situation?

He dried some leaves under the sun and rolled them into something like a cigarette. He had matches, so he lit the cigarette and started to smoke. After an hour, his throat hurt and his voice became hoarse, so he had to give up his home-made cigarettes.

And now he is standing on the beach, throwing stones into the sea, counting the number of times they skip on the water, creating tiny splashes. Often he watches the fishing boats passing by, staring at them from the time they appear to the time they disappear. He also sees the ferry boat loaded with holiday makers bound for another island. Perhaps he has also seen me, Fruits.

The ferry boat for outlying islands passes many small islands on its way, and quite by chance, it passes a desert island where its passengers see someone sunning himself on the beach. The people who see him say: What an easy life! As for the person who is sunning himself, he says: Is this the taste of leadership? The ferry boat goes relentlessly forward, casting the desert island behind. Soon, the ferry boat arrives at a bustling distant island with plenty of inhabitants.

We disembark from the ferry, walk past the bus stops where long queues have formed, and past the embankment, towards the beach. Some people are cycling on the beach embankment. The beach is filled with young people today. They are either swimming or building various sand castles. A number of young people are squatting on the main path at the beach, displaying seashells and clams in front of them. Would you like a seashell ring? or a live sea urchin? Silly looks at a sea urchin for a long while. Can you come hiking and camping with me? And how'd you fare under the sun, without water, can you take it? Silly asks the sea urchin, which does not respond. Silly then says, forget it, forget it. Anyway, you're not a camel. And so Silly has not bought a sea urchin. The shrimps in a bucket keep splashing water, making Silly's trouser legs very wet.

This beach is very wide. If you start walking from this end, you'll see cooked food stalls, some selling fish balls, noodles and stewed pig skin, others selling salted eggs and chicken wings, yet others selling sweets and cakes. After you pass these food stalls, there are shops where you can sit down and have all kinds of noodles, and also stores which sell fishing hooks and straw hats. On the embankment facing the beach there are two sturdy buildings with simple lines. One of these turns out to be a first aid station, while the other is a public lavatory.

And then you see a strange house. It is white, and you can see black and white check curtains hanging at the windows. There is a fairly big open space in front of the house, with wooden tables and chairs, and colourful umbrellas shading the tables. The house is surrounded by a white wooden fence on all four sides, and it looks like a village farmer's house.

Such a pretty house, says Silly. When he notices the flowers growing by the fence, he walks over to have a better look. It turns out that the house has several names; it calls itself Le Restaurant, also Barbecue Station, also Beer Garden. At this point, there are people scattered around a few tables in the Le Restaurant Barbecue Station Beer Garden. Over there there are three people sitting in rattan chairs, laughing and drinking lemonade and beer. Silly hears one of them say: I like the sandwiches here — no toasting, crust intact, these are sandwiches without cosmetics. Another one says: The tables and chairs here are nice too, all solid wood, no carving or brass plates or inlaid glass, these are tables and chairs without cosmetics. And another one says: I just love the space here. You can get up, turn around a couple of times, and when you sit down again, you won't be kicking at anyone's shoes.

As long as he sees that other people are happy, Silly is happy; that is why he likes to go hiking. When you are far away from the city centre, you always see a lot of smiling eyes and noses. Their faces are flushed, their clothes loose and comfortable, and their pace leisurely. What kind of faces do you see in the city centre? Sleepy eyes, mouths mumbling to themselves, loitering ears, racing legs, sweaty hands, runny noses, elbows and fists.

After we pass the beer garden, we come to a path which goes up the mountain. As we walk along this path, the beach is cast away behind our knapsacks. By the time the houses on the beach seem distant and tiny, we have come to an expanse of grassy area with a stream nearby. This is it, says Silly, and he takes his shoes off and pours a handful of sand out of them.

When everyone is setting up the tent, I help with the tent pegs, too. When everyone is lighting up the fire, I help with getting the stones, too. Come cooking time, I take the pot with the rice in it to wash in the stream. When I come back to the camp fire, there is a little fish in the pot. Since none of us objects to having fish rice, we cook the fish alongside the rice.

We are not having any vegetables. We just put tinned beef, sardines and sausages into a frying pan to cook for a while. Once they no longer look cold and dull, we tuck in. The beef is quite all right, says someone, a pity we don't have any sauces here. This rice looks more like congee, and where's that fish gone? We sit around the camp fire as we each finish a few cupfuls of rice.

To decide who'll do the washing up, we toss a coin. The loser is Tec. Tec is Merry Mak's neighbour, the one who is fond of detective stories. When everyone met up at the ferry pier, he was standing at a corner of a wall reading a detective novel. Once we got on the ferry, he sat quietly in a corner, reading his detective novel. Tec takes the pot to the river for a quick baptism, and then he comes back with the baptised pot to resume reading.

— let's go cycling

— let's go rowing

we yell. Since we have finished eating, who wants to hang around at the camp? But Tec shakes his head: I'll finish the novel first. So leaving Tec there to take care of the camp, we return to the beach along the same mountain path. When I get there, the people who ran ahead of me have already turned into fish.

At the Beer Garden there are still people scattered around several tables. The three people who like laughing are no longer sitting in the rattan chairs; they are now sitting at a wooden table under an orange-yellow umbrella, drinking coffee. One of them says: This coffee is quite all right, and the cup's colour and shape are all right, too. As he speaks, he takes another sip of coffee. Another one of them says: So, this is the world. When you observe things patiently, you will always find something good and beautiful, and these things always come about by chance and take you by surprise. And the third one says: We think this coffee is good, does the coffee know that? We think that these wooden tables and chairs without cosmetics have a natural beauty, do the tables and chairs know that?

The person who makes a sandwich with untoasted bread with crust intact is probably like an artist who paints a picture. Whether you like a picture, and whether you like a sandwich made of three pieces of bread-like bread with tomato, salad spread, eggs, bacon and ham in between, is a matter of distance between the creator and the receptor, says one of the coffee-drinkers. He is wearing a pair of cotton trousers of chestnut colour, and a cotton shirt of hay colour which blends him in completely with the coffee he is drinking.

The creator is of course important, says a coffee-drinking girl with long black hair and a face full of beautiful sunshine. And the receptor is just as important as the creator, says she.

When Merry Mak hears what these smiling people are saying, he says: I get it. It's the same business between the person who speaks into a telephone and the person who listens through the telephone.

I am not reminded of the telephone; I am suddenly reminded of concerts. In a concert, if the pianist on stage is playing well, and the audience likes the music, they applaud. And so the pianist knows that the playing is well received by the audience.

But pictures are different; no one claps his hands in front of a painting at an exhibition and exclaims: Bravo. And tables and chairs with no cosmetics are different; no one has ever applauded sandwiches or tables and chairs without cosmetics. Those who make such sandwiches and tables and chairs must feel pretty lonely.

What is more, there will always be those who run into a studio and shout: Donatello fallen among a school of wild beasts. Or they say to wooden chairs and tables: How come you all look like trees. Or they say to a sandwich: Untoasted bread is harmful to the stomach; bread with crust intact is not genteel.

At this moment, Silly is standing in the water, shouting:

— come and row

— two to a boat

And so I race across the beach, filling my shoes with sand. I get into a boat with Silly, and he gives me the paddles. It is a fine day today, with nary a wave, just foamy splashes along the edge of the beach. When a breeze comes by, the sea frowns a little, and then becomes as flat as if it has been ironed out again.

When there are no waves in the sea, rowing is easy. The boat glides forward rapidly. You can see the whirl-holes in the places where the paddles go into the water, and the water swims backwards, undulating, like a waving ribbon. It is only when I am rowing that I feel the water on the surface of the sea is not water but wool unravelled from a huge, thick scarf, wavy wool floating on the sea.

At times I row our boat far away from everyone else. Silly stirs the sea water with his hands, and hums whatever tune that takes his fancy, lalala. And so I start singing aloud, too. I know this song "Row a Boat", and every time I row I sing "Row a Boat". Row row row your boat, gently down the stream. Merrily, merrily, merrily, merrily, life is but a dream.

At times I take our boat into the midst of the other boats, and Silly says: Let's tie the boats together. So saying he stands up, clutching the edge of the boat, and walks to the front where he gets hold of a rope and ties it to the back of another boat. Soon, many boats are tied together,

— look at us

— we're like a dragon

says Silly. When the boats are all tied together, I stop rowing. Our boat glides along at the tail of other boats, and sometimes bumps into other boats, making noises, *boom, boom.* And so I put down the paddles and lay down in the boat. The sky is so blue, and the clouds look like cotton candy. Over there someone is water-skiing, the motor of a speed boat goes *ta ta ta*. The boat rolls about a little, like a cradle.

Our line squadron of boats looks like a dragon. What do dragons look like? No one has ever seen a dragon. I wonder whether they feed on grass. The dragons in picture books all look very solemn, I wonder if there is a gentle and smiling dragon. The dragons in legends are obviously intelligent and capable, I wonder if there is a fat, stupid dragon.

We do not get to see dragons nowadays. It is a great pity that there are many things which human beings do not get to see. If I were born in the year A. D. 1, I think I just might have seen Jesus. And if I did I would have told him: Your hair is very naturalistic. We all have long hair now. What would Jesus have said to that? He would certainly have told me that the Jews grew their hair long so that they would look different from the Romans. The Romans shaved closely and cut their hair short, like Greek statues. The Romans liked Greece.

Well, the Romans liked Greece, but what does that mean? You are fond of the arts, but you just turn into banging gongs and blaring trumpets, no love. What is the point of having very Greek hair and a very arty city?

And if I was born in an even earlier age, I could have met the Yellow Emperor. I like the Yellow Emperor. He was the inventor of the compass cart, and he was brave. I am proud to be a descendant of his. If I should be asked who I would like to have as an ancestor — Alexander the Great, Peter the Great, Julius Caesar or Richard the Lion-heart, I would answer: the Yellow Emperor. And I would be asked: What is so good about being a descendant of the Yellow Emperor in this place? You don't even get a passport.[1]

I do not have a passport. They say that if anyone from this place wants to travel elsewhere, not having a passport means a lot of hassle. People

---

[1] Only Hong Kong Chinese born in Hong Kong are entitled to a British Hong Kong passport. Those born in China are given Certificates of Identity (C.I.) for travelling purposes, and are often considered "stateless" by foreign governments.

from this city who do not have a passport and who want to travel must have a C.I. The C.I. is proof that you belong to this city; it is proof of your citizenship.

— What is your nationality

some people will ask, because to them all this sounds very strange. And you say: Well, well, as for nationality .... You look at your C.I. over and over again, and discover that you have no nationality, just citizenship.

The sky is so blue. The sky over this city is just as blue and as beautiful as the sky over any other city. As the sky gradually turns grey and dim, it is getting late. We have returned to the camp site and have had our dinner. We are now sitting around the camp fire. Tec is not reading his detective novel any more; he is sitting among us.

When we have all sat down, forming a circle, Tec suggests that we each give a performance: we can sing a song, or tell a horror story, as long as we each do something. And so we start with the fellow sitting next to Tec, the one who is rubbing mosquito repellent on his face. He sings a Cantonese nursery rhyme: Behind the net, behind the net, a mosquito, a mosquito. Go and get a fan, quick; go and get a fan, quick; chase it out, chase it out.[2]

In this city, when you mean the bus, you say *ba-see*;[3] when you mean fresh cream cake, you say fresh *ke-leem* cold biscuit. Since this is the case, in this city, the mouth is always quarrelling with the hand that writes. The hand says: You want me to write ice-cream, then why do you keep saying snow-cake, snow-cake? The mouth says: I'm telling you these two people are a football judge and a borderline guard, how come you write them down as referee and linesman?

---

[2] The net in the song is a mosquito net. This song is based on the tune of "Frère Jacques".

[3] The whole paragraph refers to differences between the spoken language (Cantonese) and the written language (Mandarin) used in Hong Kong. One of the major differences is vocabulary as indicated here. A large number of Hong Kong Cantonese words are transliterated English words.

The mouth and the hand that writes have been quarrelling for more than a hundred years now, so they have decided to hold a no-holds-barred public debate.

After the fellow who is rubbing mosquito repellent on his face has finished his mosquito song, the person next to him stands up. His performance is a self-introduction. He says he is a dumb fellow. There was this time when a very well-read man asked a question: What turns into a butterfly? Everyone answered: Zhuang Zi.[4] But he answered: A caterpillar.

The next performance is someone making a film. He borrows Silly's camera, puts his own sneakers on the grass, and starts shooting with great care. One minute he jumps up, the next minute he is running around, and the next minute he is lying on the grass, and as he shoots he explains that this is a freeze, that is zooming in and zooming out, and what not. At last, he has finished. He says that his sneakers will get the Oscar for best actor next year.

What follows is a riddle: A circle in the water. The fellow who gives us the riddle realizes that we are those who think caterpillars turn into butterflies, so he gives us an important clue: Think about the shape. He also says that the answer is a place in this city.

Merry Mak shouts out almost immediately. I got it, he shouts, it's Lily Pond.

Merry Mak draws a circle with a piece of charcoal, and the shape is like a pond for growing water-lilies. That's why he said Lily Pond. But the fellow who gave us the riddle shakes his head.

— it's Horns

shouts Silly. He says: put two horns together and you have a circle. The fellow shakes his head again.

— it's Fat Sha Tsui

---

[4] A famous ancient philosopher who dreamt that he had turned into a butterfly, and on waking, asked: Did I dream that I was a butterfly, or is the butterfly dreaming that it is me?

this time it is Tec shouting. Among the lot of us, Tec is the most quick-witted because he reads detective stories day and night, and because he has an enquiring spirit. Everyone applauds, thinking that Tec has cracked it. But the fellow who gave us the riddle shakes his head again. Finally, after many unsuccessful guesses, we are told the answer: Round Island.

After that, someone plays a mouth-organ, someone dances a folk dance, someone tells an absolutely unhorrifying ghost story, someone talks about the stars to the sky. One fellow talks about his life's ambition. He says: There are so many wars in the world, the best thing to do is to drive a fire engine to the battlefields to put out fires.

When Merry Mak's turn comes along, he is eating an orange, so he gives us a question about how to cut an orange. He says: Cut an orange three times to make four sections, but when you have eaten it, there should be five pieces of peel. It goes without saying that you are not to tear one piece into two, and you are not to get eight sections out of the three cuts.

All those who have oranges take them out and cut them open this way and that, so that all the oranges are peeled and eaten, but not one person has succeeded in coming up with the five pieces of peel. Finally, Silly remembers his chilies. He cuts a chili three times in circles to take off three sections, and the middle section has two pieces of peel. Silly has solved the riddle of how to cut oranges.

When a group of people are sitting together, there is always someone who suggests that each person should give a performance, and there is always someone who says I don't know how, or I have nothing to perform. Mail is like that. He says he knows no riddles, no folk dances, no apeman attack on earth. He just sits at one side. And now, since his turn has come, he points a finger at Silly, saying: You first, you first.

Silly is not afraid of performing, but his performance is a little different from the rest. It isn't singing or story-telling, and it isn't miming; it is going in search of edible fruit. Everyone approves of this, and all those who have not performed yet are to go with Silly in search of fruit. Since I have not performed anything, I go with Silly to look for fruit.

— this place

— grows great pineapples

says Silly. Torch in hand, he leads the way up the mountain path. I also have a torch. Several people are walking behind me, and Tec has come along, too. Silly has been here a number of times before, so he knows there is a pineapple field behind the mountain.

On holidays, the outlying island is wide awake even at night. We come across some tents and see people sitting in the open, singing. Some are plotting to go to nearby tents, to pinch some shoes and hang them on the trees. When we come to the peak of the mountain, we can see the distant camp fires on the beach dimly burning. These camp fires usually burn until the sky turns light again.

It is dark now, and getting late. Silly says: It's midnight. We walk along the footpath and soon come to a main road where cars rush by at frequent intervals, like one-eyed tigers. Tec says behind me: Remember black is earth white is stone shiny means puddles. I look up at the sky. There are stars up there, a net of stars.

The pineapple field is not a terraced field, nor is it a flat field. If Silly had not pointed at the slope in front of us, I would never have known that this is where the pineapples grow. At first I do not see the pineapples, just clumps of thick leaves with spikes on them. All the thick leaves follow the contours of the slope, like so many stumpy trees.

— the pineapples are sweet

— snakes love them

Tec who is walking behind me reminds me. My feet immediately tell me: We have decided to go slow. And true to their words they begin to walk carefully, step by step. Tec shines his torch on the pineapples here and there, walking around the plants to check that there are no snakes or other terrible animals. Silly has a sheath knife which he uses on the thick leaves. He then cuts at the roots on the ground, and a pineapple promptly falls into the field.

On this night there is a great hustle and bustle in the pineapple field. It turns out that the pineapples are holding an Extraordinary General

Meeting on the issue of applying to patent the word "Pineapple" so that no one will be able to take it in vain. A hundred years ago the pineapple race had patented its name once before, under the name "Phoenix Pear".

— we have to protect the reputation of pineapples

— we are fruit

one pineapple shouts.

— we are sweet and fragrant

— we are not a cocktail

shouts another pineapple.

There was this time when people in the streets all shouted: "There's a pineapple over there."[5] A few kids who heard this said at once: We like pineapples, let's go and have some. And so they all ran towards the pineapple. Strangely enough, this peculiar pineapple ended up eating the kids' mouths as well as the kids' fingers.

You see, pineapples in the street may not be real pineapples. That is why the pineapples want to protest. If you are not a poet, you are not a poet, and if you are not a pineapple, you are not a pineapple, they say.

There was this other time when two teams of people were hiding in holes on an empty site, playing hide and seek. In great excitement they ran from and ran after each other, and the game went on for a long time. Then one team said all of a sudden: Do come and have some cocktail, a very famous cocktail with a foreigner's name. It's a Molotov Cocktail. Those playing hide and seek all came up for the cocktail, and they all got very drunk, and none of them ever woke up again.

That is why the pineapples want to assert their right to their name and have it patented, because this very special cocktail is also called Pineapple.

While the pineapples are holding their E.G.M., Tec is shining his

---

[5]This refers to home-made bombs placed in the streets of Hong Kong by communist activists in their attempt to topple the Hong Kong government during the early years of the Cultural Revolution.

torch all over one pineapple, and Silly takes out his sheath knife, cutting off the hair of another pineapple. So one of them says:

— look

— someone has come to steal pineapples

That being the case, the pineapples taking part in the E.G.M. change their agenda to discuss whether they should punish the pineapple thieves. A young pineapple says: We are sweet and fragrant, and there are so many of us, just let them take some. Then they'll know that we pineapples are good fruit, that we're not some fake cocktail. Another young pineapple says: That's right. We're real pineapples; we won't eat their mouths, and we won't eat their fingers.

And so the pineapple elders deliver their opinion. They say: If the pineapple thieves have come here out of appreciation for us, and they just want to take a few of us to satisfy their palate, we will not have them punished. But if they are to take several dozen to make money out of us, we will have them punished by giving them diarrhoea for one month. The decision made, they say to the three pineapples which have been chopped off by Silly: Brothers, go and be our goodwill ambassadors, go and restore the good name of the pineapple.

Altogether we dig up three pineapples to take back to the camp. They are the sweetest and most fragrant pineapples I have ever had.

Come next morning, we are too lazy to cook, so we make some noodles called "Two-and-a-half Minutes". We wrap our shoes round our socks, and we wrap our socks round our feet, then we put on our clothes, take down the tent and fold it up. Mail takes the pot to the stream to get some water which he pours on the camp fire to put it out. Then everyone takes part in a short clean-up campaign, putting all the waste paper, tins and plastic bags into a rubbish bin. After that, with the hot sun over our heads, we walk along a mountain path to the next small town, Chung Town. We are not climbing the mountain; we just walk one behind the other, trailing a string of colours on the mountain path.

— I like the sky in this city

someone shouts in front. Someone else walking in front moos like a cow, and another person plays the mouth-organ for a short while. The sky overhead is very blue, as blue as yesterday. And because the sky is blue, the trees look very green. The distant hills have all turned purple, like rising black fog. Only the grass and trees near us are green, dotted with off-white and yellow.

— I like the sea in this city

someone else shouts. It is also someone walking in the front. All those who are walking in the front are stumping along, making the gravel on the path crackle under their feet. Occasionally some gravel falls down the slope. When someone mentions the sea, it occurs to everyone how nice it would be if we could jump into the water for a swim. All our clothes are wet.

I turn to look at the mountain path we have travelled along. The pineapple field is hidden behind tall trees, and at frequent intervals houses can be glimpsed between the chinks of the branches. On the distant sea, a ferry for the outlying islands is coming this way.

— I like the roads in this city

says Mail. When Mail says he likes the roads here, he begins to talk about other roads. He says he has seen dirt tracks where there is nothing but dirt. On fine days the dirt is dry, so when a vehicle drives past the dust flies to a height of a seven- or eight-storeyed building. All the pedestrians become vacuum cleaners. On rainy days the dirt track turns into a trap, dragging down your feet like ghosts. Dirt tracks are terrible, says Mail.

And now Silly begins to speak, too. He says he has seen a kind of road made of pebbles. It looks beautiful. The whole road is pebbles; when people walk on it, it looks as if they are walking on a stream.

However, pity the car that runs on the pebble road. Whoever sits in the car would think he is in a fun park's bumper car. Silly says: The pebble road is a very old road, and like so many ancient things which no longer suit the needs of today, it still makes us nostalgic, the same way that horse-drawn carriages, candles, canoes and castles do.

Then suddenly Tec speaks up at the end of the line. He likes to observe plants and flowers closely, and he is collecting some peculiarly-shaped leaves to take home as specimens. He has even picked a huge yellow flower from a cactus, and as a result his thumb has been pricked by a thorn. As for roads, Tec says that he knows of a kind of road which is very beautiful too; it's a road paved with colourful tiles forming patterns of flowers, vases, and various other pictures.

Will our city also have a main road paved with pictures? If we make paintings out of street tiles, then we will have a street art exhibition every day. And if that is the case, there will be many more places in the city where we can take a stroll.

It is noon when we get to Chung Town. We are here to see an old fortress with its ancient cannons. We eat our fill of noodles in the small shop next to the Chung Town pier, sit around for the time it takes to smoke two cigarettes, and head for the old fortress.

One after another we rush into the fortress. We run through an arched door, up a flight of stairs and on to the fortress wall. Everyone is excited at the sight of the cannons lining the wall. Mail is the first to walk over to bid the cannons a very good afternoon. Silly is busy taking pictures of everybody. Merry Mak says: This cannon looks exactly like a huge red chili. The cannon must be really hot. I turn to take a brief look at the stairs behind us, and when I turn back I see five or six people already sitting on a cannon.

I see a square in the middle of the fortress, like a tennis court. There is a big tree next to the square, and some people are kicking a ball around in the square. I see a row of battlements along the edge of the fortress wall. I see grains of sand in the earth on the wall, and some weeds growing there. I see that the body of the cannon is like a king-size biscuit tin. I see two low stone walls built on either side of a cannon, each as tall as a child. I see every cannon is aimed at the plain in front of us.

Tec, who is standing beside me, has pulled out from his pocket a map with words written on it. He points here and there, and I have no idea whether he is talking to me, or talking to himself. All I hear him say is: This fortress is old. This fortress is two hundred years old. Now who was the emperor at that time? I must look it up in the history books when I get home.

At this time, besides us, there are many other people on the fortress wall. All these people have also come here to have a look at the fortress. Some of them have come by ferry, some by hired boats, some by bus. And now they are all on the fortress wall. They have also climbed up onto the cannons. Each group is laying seige to one cannon.

As so many people are laying seige to a cannon, they are bound to question the cannon. They ask: Cannon, are you made of bronze? They ask again: Cannon, will you suddenly start firing again and make a loud noise some day?

After this person asked the cannon whether it would suddenly start firing and make a loud noise, he continues to ask questions. But this time the questions are not directed at the cannon, they are directed at his friends: If the cannon should start firing again, what would you do? Would you run away, or would you stand by this city?

At this moment yet another group of young people have come to see the fortress. One of them is skipping up the stairs with a happy smile on his face, singing a song. What he is singing is:

If you're going to San Francisco

Be sure to wear some flowers in your hair

As soon as he comes up to the fortress wall and sees the cannons, he says: What a beautiful cannon! In his hand is a bunch of wild flowers of various shapes and colours, and he sticks it into the cannon's mouth.

 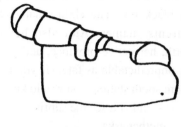

— and what did you see there
mother asks.

Mother is sitting in a rocking-chair. I tell her I saw cannons. I saw cannons lining the fortress wall. When the time comes for them to go off, I believe they will shake the whole city. I tell her that the cannons I saw were black in colour. Although it is summer, and it was noon, they were warm to the touch, like a sleeping volcano. Though there seemed to be boiling lava inside, the volcano was asleep.

The cannons mother had known were not warm, they were red hot. The cannons mother had known were not sleeping volcanos, they were wide awake. Those cannons blasted basin-shaped holes in the Olympic stadium; those cannons turned a whole plain of peach blossoms into scorching flames. At the railway station the whole floor was littered with single shoes. (If you had come from south station, you would know.)

A mother called out the name of a little girl. The girl was carrying her own little bag on her back, with her clothes and a few days' rations inside. Sewn to her clothes was a square of white cloth on which names were written in black ink. The child's name, and her parents' names. And also her date of birth, her native province, and an address as unpredictable as fate. (If you had come from south station, you would know.)

— did you see the sunrise
mother asks.

I did not. I did not go up the mountain to see the sun rise. That was because the sky had darkened. I can never predict my own fortune. When we left the ancient fortress, we said goodbye to the group of cannons and took a path that goes up another mountain. We walked on for four whole hours. It started to rain. It was a drizzle, like a wet net hanging over our heads. It was because of the rain that we did not go up to a higher peak to see the sunrise.

Looking at the sunrise is like searching for hope, mother says. Those who go to see the sunrise always get up at shortly after three in the morning. All around them is a blur of emptiness. They group together, flashlights in hand, and follow the leader on the trek up the mountain. Though they all have thick clothes on, they still say: Oh, it's so cold. And it is August, the height of summer.

Everyone waits on the peak. If it is a peak surrounded by mountain ranges, and the clouds in the distance brighten first, you would think that these are the colours of sunset. When all the clouds are aglow with bright colours, suddenly, there is the sun, floating in a mountain gorge.

No one can make out the shape of the sun, whether it is round or square; its brilliance is so dense and so blinding that no one can take a good look at it. All one has is a feeling of what the sun looks like. It is like a rapidly revolving, brilliant colour mixer.

Mother likes the sunrise on the ocean. A morning on the embankment, looking at the white sky, so white it was almost transparent. It was already dawn, around six in the morning. A white ball rose out of the distant sea. All of a sudden it shot up from the water as though it had kicked its way out, whipping up a considerable spray. Or perhaps it was like someone taking a dumpling out of a bowl of sweet soup. The white ball was not bright at all; it was rather like snow, or a lump of dough ready for the oven. The white ball was also like the moon rising slowly from the ocean: a series of stills run together. The white ball floating in the sky was so fragile, so pale, and then suddenly it shone forth with the utmost brilliance, and the eye could see it no more.

I did not see the sunrise. We camped on a sizable piece of flat land on the peak. That day we cooked some vegetables which we had picked from the fields we walked past. We also picked some papayas. It was drizzling, and we took a stroll. In the tea fields nearby, the tea shrubs stretched out many tiny twigs. The new tea leaves washed by the rain were like fresh green vegetables, but the old tea leaves were dark.

— what else did you see

asks mother.

Mother gently fans herself with a straw fan. I tell her I saw the convicts. They had on dark blue tops and shorts, and some were naked from the waist up. They were working on the road. I saw them planting trees — digging holes, and then putting the seedlings into the earth. I saw them paving the road, pushing a two-handled wheelbarrow.

When we came down the mountain we walked along the catchwater into a forestation area where there were no roads, and we almost got lost. There were so many trees, their many leaves could have made up a thick specimen album.

I do not remember how we came out of the forestation area. It was a maze, but it was beautiful. If I had not been able to make my way out, I would have had no regrets. Yet we saw the path outside, charged towards it, and out we came. We walked past a prison, a no-security one. The convicts were working near the catchwater. As we watched them work, some of them asked: Got any cigarettes? Those who did offered them all their cigarettes, and they lit up at once. When they were given cigarettes, they said thank you to us.

Mother recalls two faces. When she walked out of a bakery, she was holding a long stick of bread. Before she had walked down to the end of the street, a black hand appeared before her eyes, grabbed the bread, and disappeared. She looked at the empty paper bag in her hand, dazed for a while. Then she began to look around for the hand that took the bread away. She saw a small, thin man standing next to a lamp post in front of her. He had on a cap which covered his messy hair and a good half of his face, and he stared hard at her with black eyes that seemed to be falling out.

That man, he did not run away, he just stood under the street lamp, rapidly stuffing bread into his mouth, and wolfing it down. The bread was so white, his eyes looked even blacker. Holding a small end of bread in his hand, the man stood under the street lamp, staring at her. (If you had come from south station, you would have known hunger.)

Another time there was a haggard man standing at a street corner. When she walked past him, alone, he said: Give me your purse. And Mother's hand that was holding onto the purse suddenly became empty. She asked: How am I to live then? The haggard man opened the purse and took all the money out. She looked at his face, which was like an old chopstick. It was a heavily lined face, his eyebrows and mouth looked liked straw baskets turned upside down.

How am I to live then? I'm hard up enough as it is, she said. He glanced at her, his sad face all wrinkled up. He took two of the banknotes, put the rest back into the purse, returned it to her, and left in a hurry. (If you had come from south station, you would have known poverty.)

If you had lived in Fisherman Harbour, you would have known violence. A young man, mouth full of chewing gum, said: Oh, so this miserable pittance is all you got? You'll get a taste of my knife then.

— did you see the temple
mother asked.

Mother had seen temples. There was this temple, she says, which had no beams. It was a strangely beautiful piece of architecture. The temple was made entirely of brick, from the ground to the roof. The roof was arched, like a bridge. There were no beams in the temple. When you looked up, you just saw the curves of the arches, one after another. If you stood in the middle of the main hall and looked up at the roof, you could see a skylight. It was just a hole.

There was a temple with a mountain cliff in front of it. A stream singing merrily in front of the mountain, and there were a large number of Buddha statues on the cliff. Some people said that this mountain had flown there from somewhere else. After just one night, there it was, with the statues of Buddha, and the stream at its foot. Those who came to see the mountain liked to go into the cave. They looked up at a small hole in the cave-roof where sunlight comes through from who knows where. They could see a bit of sky from the cave.

I saw the temple. When we woke up in the morning, it was still drizzling. We folded up our tents. We had some dry rations for breakfast. And then we went to see the temple. We saw smoke in the temple. Bunches of incense sticks were burning in the incense burner. There were many stalls around the temple, selling fragrant wood with healing powers, rosaries, and edible peas.

Silly said why don't we go and ask for a sign. He produced a bunch of incense sticks out of nowhere, stuck them into the incense burner, held onto the spill holder with both hands, and knelt down on a prayer mat. He shook the spill holder hard, *clack, clack*, and soon spills fell to the ground. The first time there were two. Silly picked them up, put them back into the holder, and shook again. This time he shook out one spill.

— what did you pray for
everyone asked.
— god bless my city
he said.

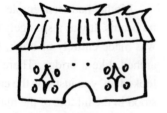

14

(Fruits, wouldn't it be marvellous if we could shout at each other on the phone for a while.)

Swim has been in Houston for five days now. Swim likes life at sea; Swim likes ships. I'd like to see all four corners of the world, Swim said. When Swim was attending classes together with Fruits, he always had a geography textbook on his desk, no matter what class it was. There were postcard style pictures in the geography book. Pyramids, camels; the Congo, lions; Brazil, football. The book said: It is hot in the Congo. Hot, how hot? Swim did not know.

— I must feel it for myself

It was then that Swim made his decision. Swim likes the wandering life, and so he threw away his books. When Fruits played football in the school playground, Swim sat in a corner taking apart electric lamps, electric fans, fridges and ovens, and then putting them back together. When Fruits studied at home for school tests, Swim enrolled in a night school to study projects to do with electrical appliances. When Fruits had to cut down on swimming because of the school certificate exam, Swim said farewell to the school, and started working for a shipping company. Swim became ship's electrician. Swim likes ships.

This is a harbour, where ships come every day. Some ships come to unload their goods, to get supplies, to stock up on water; others come here for repairs or for a new coat of paint. Different ships flying different flags. The ships need a major overhaul once every seven years, and a minor one once every four. And so the ships come to this harbour for checkups. Without their health certificates, ships cannot go to sea.

Swim learned how to give ships their checkups. He picked up from his colleagues various kinds of knowledge about electrical equipment on ships, such as wiring, installing electricity meters, engine maintenance, checking voltage, repairing generators, and putting in fuseboards.

After Fruits took the school certificate exam, he received a high school graduation certificate. After Swim had served his two-year apprenticeship on board ship, he received a reference certificate and a red passbook[1] from the Port Authority. He also received an eighteen-month contract from a shipping company and one month's salary in advance known to sailors as "family maintenance pay". Swim handed over fifty percent of the salary to his mother and kept the other fifty percent. He bought two thick coats and six new sets of underwear. He packed all the things he needed, including an old quilted jacket, a few reference books on electrical equipment, a world map, a camera, a tape-recorder, and boarded an aeroplane called seven something seven.

— start a stamp collection

Swim said to Fruits. On the plane Swim took out his world map and pored over it. He wanted to go to all four corners of the world. He drew a circle around the port where he had started off. I expect this map will end up covered with circles and lines, he thought. Swim had four companions on his flight. They were sailors, he an electrician.

Seated in front of Swim were two young men. Swim had no idea where they were going, or whether they were students or workers. He only heard them say: Now we're rid of this dirty overpopulated suffocating city. I swear I'll never come back.

Swim watched as the harbour underneath him receded. And then it was an expanse of white ocean. Goodbye, Swim said, My beloved

---

[1] A Hong Kong registered sailor's proof of identification.

beautiful and ugly city. And so Swim opened his map.

The aeroplane flew over a mountain, circling it twice. Swim could see the snow covering it. Dusk was falling and the sun was setting. From the plane, Swim saw that streets were like neatly marked fields. When the plane landed at Tokyo airport, Swim and his sailor friends waited in the transit lounge for their connecting flight. He saw the young men who sat in front of him, and all of a sudden they asked him in English: Are you Japanese?

Swim changed planes several times. He flew via Honolulu, Hawaii and Massachusetts before finally arriving in Houston.

(Fruits, This is my first postcard to you. The black stone on the picture looks very commonplace, like a lump of coal. It is a rock from the moon.

This is the exhibition room in the Space Centre. The walls are lined with pictures and the floor is covered with a white carpet. I saw the slide show. Fruits, wouldn't it be marvellous if we could go travelling to the moon.)

Swim finally laid eyes on the ship he had been waiting for. It is a Panamanian cargo ship with her name on the stern: the *Oriental*. Her hull is black, the decks red, the bridge white, and the chimney yellow and blue. When Swim saw her, the ship was docked on Houston River.

This ship has been in service for two years, and there are many people on board. Swim goes on board to report to duty where he met the captain and the first mate. All those on board are Chinese; some are graduates of nautical colleges and others plain sailors.

The Oriental had come from New Orleans with an empty hold for a cargo of fertilizer. A thick conveyor belt stretches on to the ship from a warehouse close to the sea, and in a fury of noise fills the ship with seventeen thousand tons of fertilizer. When Swim gets on board, he watches the lumps of fertilizer, round and black like coal, fall into the cargo hold. Fertilizer looks like moon rocks, Swim thinks.

Swim has his own room. In the room there is a bed, a wardrobe and a couch, all of which are bolted to the wall. Even if the ship should sway with all its might, these pieces of furniture would always stay in position. Swim also has a desk with one big drawer and four small drawers. The desk has a glass top. Swim puts his sixty-six-pound luggage on the floor, opens his world map and puts it under the glass top. This map now boasts the addition of a few circles and a red line zig-zagging through them. So, I'm as far away from my native city as this, says Swim. I wonder if mother has received my letters yet.

— are there any letters

As the *Oriental* docked on Houston River and new crew came on board, everyone came out with this question mark.

— and how is our city

— is it doing OK

again they ask.

Swim and his companions hand the letters over to the crew. They have also brought them news of the city in the form of some newspapers, magazines, weekly newspapers and periodicals. Everyone crowds together, reading eagerly. So many robberies, those reading the newspapers shake their heads and sigh. So many refugees, what are we to do? Someone tears a newspaper into two halves, takes one page and stands in a corner to read.

Those who have not managed to get hold of newspapers surround Swim and the new crew members who came on board with him. Tell us some news. What was the city like when you left, they ask. And so Swim tells them whatever he knows.

Many refugees have come. Some came in their dozens, by aeroplane, and they have all left now. Some came by boat, in their thousands. Those who came by plane stayed in a camp in town. Those who came by boat stayed in a camp in the countryside.

There are tents and bungalows in the camps, surrounded by barbed wire fences. People line both sides of the barbed wire fences from morning till night. Many people have come here to look for relatives, and their eyes fall on every face. Those who succeed in finding their relatives stand outside the barbed wire fences, talking to them.

— we will do our best

— we will make application for you

they say. It is ten o'clock at night, and they are still standing there. Other people are also standing outside the fences. They are not here to look for relatives, and they are not reporters. They just walk back and forth outside the fences, whispering to the people inside:

— anything to exchange?

— watches?

Occasionally they take a watch through a hole in the fence. Thirty dollars, they say. A jewellery shop a long way from the camp has suddenly become very busy — within one day it has exchanged a large quantity of gold worth tens of thousands of dollars. The gold was all in taels.

On the day a refugee boat got to the city, a woman gave birth on board. After the boat was berthed, the baby was taken to hospital for a medical checkup. When the baby was fit enough to be discharged, the hospital said: Would the mother please come for her baby. However, no one turned up to collect the baby.

In the camp each person is allocated a bed; some are allocated canvas beds. They open up the canvas and pull the eyelets on both sides of the wooden frame. They each have a pair of chopsticks and a tin bowl. They line up for meals every day. There is a huge room where they can choose their clothes. The room is filled with clothes, and they can take as many as they please.

One family made a pledge to heaven. They said that if they could leave this city alive they would become vegetarian for so many years. Thereupon, they poured a lot of soy sauce into their rice.

There is a man, called Papillon. He hid himself in a rice barrel. The rice they eat every day is put in a barrel as tall as a table. To loosen up the rice you need a navvy's shovel. After every meal, the camp workers collect all the barrels onto a truck and transport them back to where they came from. One day they found Papillon hiding in one of the barrels. The truck was on the road when Papillon lifted the barrel cover and stood up. He was put into solitary confinement and was given a ration of plain rice and water. After one day, they saw him scaling the fence. This is a butterfly which cannot fly.[2]

On the *Oriental* there are two electricians; one is called senior Sparks, the other junior Sparks. The electricians' job is to take care of all things related to electricity on board ship. When senior Sparks says, Come with me, Swim follows him. When senior Sparks says, Go and check out the generator, Swim goes to check out the generator.

His working day starts at six-thirty in the morning. After Swim gets up, he does the round of all corridors, public areas, and passageways to see if the lights are all right. On board ship, all lights are left on day and night. After Swim has taken a look at all the lights, he returns to his own room. That is usually about seven o'clock. At seven, the waiter comes. He knocks on the door and then comes in to ask: What would you like for breakfast?

After breakfast, Swim continues his work. And so he goes to the lower deck to look at the electricity switch-board. By the side of the switch-board there is a small box, and Swim must check to see if there are any memos left in the box — those would be the work instructions senior Sparks leaves for him. The memos would tell him what needs to be repaired, and what needs to be checked. When Swim gets these memos, he follows the instructions on them, takes care of all the repairs, signs the memos, and deposits them in another box.

Around this time, Swim also has to check the ship's generator. He usually tests its temperature with his hand.

He also has to see to the ventilation system, the fire alarm lights and the alarm system. If everything is in order and there are no special appliances to be repaired, for Swim the morning's work is done.

All the crew members on the *Oriental* are Chinese. Half of them are Chinese who speak Mandarin, the other half Chinese who speak Cantonese. On this ship, there are more young people than old ones. There

---

[2]Papillon is French for butterfly and the hero of a well known film about prisoners in a French penal colony.

are many who have come from the same city as Swim, and in their spare time, they always ask: Are there many more buildings in our city? Are there many more people? Those who ask these questions have been away from the city for two years. Two years can see a lot of changes in a city. Swim always answers their every question.

There have been many refugees, says Swim. Some of them climbed over many mountains; they came in their tens of thousands over hill and dale, all heading in the same direction. Some of them wore cloth shoes, others plastic slippers, others were bare-footed. It did not matter what type of feet they had, they all had blisters.

When countless people were moving towards the city like a mobile forest, crowds in the city were hastening towards the mountains. They took with them food and water. In the mountains, you would suddenly hear people cry out: Is that you, mother? Is that you, brother? And then there was silence.

Among those who went up to the mountains, only a small number were looking for their relatives. Others who brought food and water just spoke kindly to those who walked up to them: You must be hungry. You foot is hurt. And so they put medication on bleeding wounds and gave food to starving bodies. Many clothes and shoes were put on by complete strangers.

There were others who came via the sea. They came in small groups of three or four, or they came alone. Since they were afloat on the sea, no one could go and say to them: You must be hungry. They spent days and nights at sea. On their way here, some of their bodies were half eaten by sharks; others had started rotting. By the time they arrived at the beaches of this city, their faces were unrecognizable, their bodies no longer whole.

When Swim comes out of the smoking room, he has finished the morning's work and he can now go back to his own room and rest. He can sleep some more, or read, or write letters. But Swim does not do any of this; he just stands on deck. He wants to have a good look at the ship on which he is standing.

This is a huge cargo ship. The space below deck is now filled with fertilizer. This ship is bound for Argentina. Swim has little idea what the ship's first port of call will be. He always thought that the first foreign country he would see would be Mexico. Swim likes Mexico. He used to say to all his classmates: Amigo, amigo. Amigo means friend. But Argentina is fine. Swim likes Argentina, too; he likes all Latin American countries. Amigo, amigo.

Standing on deck, Swim can see the ocean. The ocean is all around him. The ocean that is close to the ship is ocean, the ocean that is far away is sometimes ocean, sometimes sky. Swim can see fish flying out of the water, and then falling back into the water. Sometimes a flower in brilliant red and green appears on the ocean. Just as Swim wonders why such a strange flower should grow on the sea, attracting sea birds to it, the flower sinks under water. It turns out to be a strange fish swimming upside down.

(Fruits, I wish I knew what you are doing now. Is your work interesting? Too bad that even if you write to me, it will be hard for me to get your letters. The ship is in a different place every day.)

I am sitting in a classroom, reading the postcard from Swim. In the daytime, I lay telephone lines in the streets. In the evening, once a week, I come to this classroom to attend a class. This is a class offered by the technical college and designed specifically for workers at the telephone company. Anyone who wants to know more about telephones can come. I would like to know more, so here I am.

The lecturer is a foreigner. He is always smiling during class, as though it is not really a class, as though we have all come for a chat. He always wears sandals, knee-high socks, shorts, and a T-shirt. The first time he came into the classroom he said to us: Don't worry if you are a bit late, the important thing is to come every time.

Those who come to class work in various departments in the telephone company in the daytime. After a full day's work, they are obviously tired in the evening. That being the case, sometimes someone yawns. Others put their heads on the desk and rest before the lecturer comes in. This is the time when I read and re-read Swim's postcards. I also look at the patterns and colours on the stamps. Besides postcards, Swim also sends letters — page after page of writing, like a diary.

During the break, the garden patio at the stern becomes very crowded. In this garden there are green leaves, and there are flowers. They tell Swim that the plant with big leaves and small flowers is begonia. Swim remembers his geography; that was his best subject in school. Begonia, our country is the shape of a begonia leaf. Swim remembers. You may speak Mandarin, or you may speak Cantonese; on the map our country looks like a begonia leaf.

There are some deck chairs on the garden patio. Sitting in a deck chair looking at the expanse of ocean in the distance, Swim feels that it is exactly like lying on the beach when he went swimming.

Except that here, he can see fish leaping out of the water, looking like rain. The fish sparkle silvery white, as brilliant as the shimmering waves.

Swim can see seagulls and terns. The terns are black, their feet are webbed like ducks' feet. Some of the sailors gather in the garden to chat, others are playing their favourite card games in the kitchen. A couple of sailors are still reading old newspapers, as though the news reported in them is as fresh as milk.

The news in these papers is old by now. Take that ship which rescued some three thousand refugees from the sea. When the ship sailed into the harbour of one big city, the city said: We don't have enough food; we are suffering from a water shortage; we don't have enough housing; half our population is unemployed. The ship quietly left with all its refugees, uttering not a word.

The ship sailed to many cities, all of which turned a sad face to it. Some cities shut their gates. And so the ship had nowhere to berth, and the people on it had nowhere to go. Go to another city, said City A. Get out of here, said City B. And so the ship left. No one knows where the ship finally went. Vessels at sea never spotted it, and none of the cities ever saw it again. There was no news, no sign of it. A ship filled with refugees went out to sea and then disappeared; that is old news.

For Swim, everything is taken care of on board; he does not have to
spend a cent on food or clothing. I can save up all my money, Swim thinks.
If I do that I may be able to have a small café in the future. And if I have
even more money, I can open a bookstore next to the café. And if these
turn out to be profitable, I'll open a cinema on the other side of the café.
When Fruits comes for coffee, it will be on the house. When Fruits comes
to see a film, it will be on the house. Whatever book Fruits would like to
have, he can have it. The café will be open for business from morning till
night, and the walls will be hung with paintings. The café will look like
a ship, thinks Swim.

Swim is happy. He is confident that he will have a café in the future.
Didn't he use to say that he would travel the world, that he would sail the
seas? Now he is on board a ship which is going to Latin America, to
Africa, to Europe. He doesn't see why he shouldn't have a café in the
future.

Swim's neighbour across the corridor is the ship's carpenter. On his
way to the cookhouse for breakfast, as soon as Swim stepped out of his
room, he came across the carpenter who put one podgy hand on the door
frame and nodded at him by way of greeting.

— you are junior Sparks, aren't you

— I am Carpenter

said he. He speaks Mandarin, and Swim doesn't. Carpenter mimed a
few movements — the gestures of planing wood, hammering a nail —
and then he pointed at tables and chairs. Swim understood him.

Every day Swim walks past Carpenter's room a few times, and every
time he can see Carpenter listening to his portable radio; occasionally
Carpenter would be doing paper-cutting. When Swim walks past his door,
Carpenter says: Come in and have a chat. And so Swim goes in.
Carpenter's room is the same as Swim's, except that on his walls there
are colourful paper-cuttings. When Swim goes into Carpenter's room for
a chat, Carpenter treats him to a soft drink.

Swim has never seen Carpenter plane wood, and he has never seen
him repair the stairs or make new windows. When Carpenter goes to

work, he always comes back in no time, and he never takes any hammers or nails with him. Because of this, Swim asks him:

— are you really a carpenter

Carpenter points at himself, saying: Carpenter. Swim looks at the doors, windows, beds and chairs in the ship; all these wooden fixtures have been made together with the ship. Doors and windows are unlike electrical appliances — could it be that Carpenter, like Swim, goes to check on all the staircases and memos every day? And so Swim asks:

— what do you do

— on board this ship

Carpenter has a pair of scissors in his hand. He picks up a piece of coloured paper with his other hand and soon he cuts out a fish. It is a fish complete with scales and eyes. He holds the fish at a distance, stretching his arm out as long as it will go, and looks at his paper fish. Light filters through the tiny cut-out holes. Carpenter feels that there is something not quite right about the fish, so he takes it back and starts cutting again. When Swim asks him: what do you do on board this ship, he shows Swim the fish: I make paper-cuttings, he says. After a while, he studies Swim's eyes and nose.

— I take care of the cats on the ship

says he. How come there are cats on the ship? When Swim was in school he had been fond of cartoons. There were frequently ships in cartoons, and people on the pier waving goodbye to those on the ships. Those on board would throw down streamers and ribbons, and people on the pier would hold on to one end of these ribbons. Soon the ship starts its journey. At this moment, Swim sees a group of rats in a cartoon similarly bidding each other farewell. A few of the rats board the ship too by way of a cable tying the ship to the pier.

But where are the cats? Swim asks. Carpenter takes Swim to have a look at them. Carpenter leads Swim on to the deck and takes him to the bow of the ship. When they get to the bow, Carpenter points at a black object attached to thick chains lying under the mast. Swim can see that what is on the floor is an anchor.

— I take care of the kedge

— to make sure it doesn't rust

says Carpenter. Swim looks at the kedge, then at Carpenter. Carpenter has jet black hair and jet black eyes, the same as Swim. However, Carpenter does not speak Swim's language, nor Swim Carpenter's. Both of them have to gesticulate, as though they are dumb. I'd like to learn to speak Mandarin, says Swim to Carpenter. Carpenter says, Good. And so Swim takes Mandarin lessons with Carpenter every day.

Carpenter teaches Swim Mandarin; he also tells Swim many things about the ship. And so Swim comes to learn about Carpenter's job — taking care of the anchors as well as measuring the supply of drinking water on board. Four times a day — early morning, noon, afternoon and at night — Carpenter goes to measure the supply of drinking water. How much has been consumed, how much is left, that is what Carpenter has to check. He lowers a string till it reaches the surface of the water in the tank, and then draws it up. Water is stored in the tanks on both sides of the ship. Beneath the water tanks are the oil tanks.

(Fruits, it'd be so nice if you could meet my friend Carpenter too. He taught me to make paper-cuttings today. Now I know how to cut apples. I'm sending you one. What do you think of it.)

15

For a while now we have not been laying telephone lines in the streets. Instead, we have been going into people's homes to repair telephones. Every day, we go back to the exchange to sign the register, then we call the repairs headquarters. Where should we go to do repairs, we ask them. Then they give us the addresses, and off we go to repair the phones.

Merry Mak always walks in front of me. He is the one to ring the doorbell. People who come to answer the door always ask: Who is it. Telephone repairs, says Merry Mak, and he shows them his staff identity card. A heavy iron gate then opens nosily.

We always ask: What's wrong with the phone. They always answer: It's dead. Or: It's turned into a radio and is playing music. And so we throw our canvas bags down on the floor and go over to see why the telephone refuses to provide good service.

I know nothing about repairs; Merry Mak is the one who shows me how everything is done. He walks over to a corner of the wall, locates a black box which he opens to reveal the wires. He then clips onto the wire a special handset designed for listening only. After listening to it for a while, he gives it to me so that I can listen to it, too. I hear a noise that goes *du du du*. Merry Mak says: That means the street phone line is working fine, so it must be the indoor line that's faulty.

Merry Mak then carefully checks the telephone lines in the flat. He always manages to locate the section that is unwell. Most of the time the plastic coating of this section is missing, revealing the copper wires inside. As the copper wires come into contact with other objects, they suddenly transmit voices from other people's telephone conversations, or equally suddenly they connect you to a song, or just as suddenly they chatter noisily and incomprehensibly.

Once, I heard a telephone say: There is no beginning and no end to human existence. Do you think that I will cease to exist when I die? But I will be everywhere. I will be part of history; I will be part of past experience; I will be a bridge between the past and the future.

After it said all this, the telephone sang a few bars of a song. And then it went on to say: The purpose of modern education is to turn every person into an encyclopaedia. If you are not intelligent, efficient, clever, always right, mechanically precise and computer accurate, what then are you doing in this world?

After saying this, the telephone sang some more. Finally, it said: The fact that you don't like photosynthesized images does not make you a pastoral poet. After this, the telephone went dead. I shook it, but it refused to say a word. I frequently come across telephones like this. Listening to telephones saying all the strange things they want to say is almost a daily experience for me.

When we go out to repair telephones, we come across all sorts of people. Some think that we are thieves, and they keep a close watch on us. Others think that we are members of a circus, and they put their heads into our canvas bags to see whether a lion would come out of it. When they see that all we take out of the bags is telephone wires, they look obviously disappointed.

Many people like to treat us to soft drinks. On average we repair at least ten telephones a day, and so we would have ten soft drinks a day. If we come across people making sweet red bean soup, they offer us red bean soup.

When the ship makes its way across the equator, the midday sun is shining directly overhead. It is extremely hot; even the breeze feels like it has been cooked. On the surface of the ocean there is a layer of white vapour. The water on the sea looks especially calm, like a pane of glass. The freezer room on board is cold, and all the food is stored there. Besides the freezer room, the ship's canteen is also air-conditioned. When the people who have been sitting in the canteen come out into the open air, they all sneeze and catch colds. Everyone on board is sweating profusely. The sweat runs into their eyes, and their eyes begin to smart.

When the ship crosses the equator, the temperature of the engine room rises from the normal 130° to 170°. Swim takes a shower every two hours, but even the water is warm. Carpenter has a cycad in his room, and when the ship crosses on the equator, a flower actually blooms on the cycad.

On the few nights when the ship sails across the equator, Swim has squid congee. The seamen caught the squid themselves. When the ship left Houston, it passed through Tampa where it anchored off shore. At night 500-watt lights were turned on to illumine the sea. On one side of the ship a gangway was lowered, and three men stood on it, each holding a net. The fish from the fridge, no longer fresh, were thrown into the sea, together with left over bread crumbs. And so the squid started coming. They looked very white, and when they swam they slid forward and then they slid back, as if they were performing some kind of dance. When they got caught in the nets, they sprayed black ink, staining everyone on the gangway. Now that the ship is sailing on the equator, these squid have turned into ingredients for congee.

The ship sailed past Tampa, past Cuba, and skirted Panama. Swim saw that the sea there was dotted with yachts and fishing boats. And then the ship passed the West Indies and Trinidad, sailing along Brazil's long coastline, past El Salvador. At this moment the ship is at Santos, replenishing its oil and drinking water supply. As Swim stands on deck, he can see a distant city floating in the black night. It is a city on the sea, decorated with numerous lights. Is it my city? Is it my city? Swim cries out loud. All of a sudden he is under the impression that he has returned to the city where he lived.

There are countless beaches along the coast of Brazil. They all look like bats stretching their wings. As the ship dropped anchor in Santos, a long and narrow oil boat came up to the *Oriental*; the logo of the oil company was painted on the boat. Another boat came with drinking water, water which had been chlorinated.

When the ship's oil tank was being filled up, the kitchen was not in use. Smokers were not allowed to smoke. After two hours, the ship has drunk its fill of oil, stored enough water, and stocked up on fresh fruit. It heads southward again.

Sometimes there are big waves at sea. The waves pound on the bow, and the ship rolls left and right as it moves forward. Those who eat in the canteen all put a wet towel on the table to prevent the dishes from sliding to the floor when the ship rolls.

Some of the new crew members become sick. Everyone tells them to stop drinking tea with milk, to lie down more frequently. Now the whole ship is rolling violently, and the drinking water has turned murky. The water in the water tanks has been completely shaken up; all the impure sediment has disappeared.

Swim is not feeling seasick. He notices that some people can still play mahjongg in the common room. Though the wooden shelves, tables and chairs in the common room are all bolted to the floor, the mahjongg tiles are not. Yet they stand firmly on the table; none had fallen to the floor.

Many rooms on board are equipped with watertight doors which are closed when the sea turns rough. Swim does not like being confined in a room; he prefers to stand somewhere safe outside to look at the sea. He watches as the waves lift the ship off the surface of the ocean. Where the sea is deep, the water is blue; where it is shallow, the water is green.

Swim has not come across many days of rough seas. Most days the sea is like an expanse of half-liquid bean curd. As the ship moves forward, ripples in the shape of an inverted V stretch endlessly. Swim has seen many fish. Sharks are fond of swimming in circles close to the ship. Devilfish have tails, and when they soar above the sea water they look like kites. Dolphins come in schools, like herds of sheep in the ocean. Huge hawksbill turtles swim together in their dozens, like ducks.

Swim opens his map. He draws a big circle around one particular place. The name: Buenos Aires. Swim looks at the map. This is Argentina, a country in the shape of a long crocodile tail, a country which occupies 35 degrees of the southern hemisphere's longitude. Argentina, at last! says Swim.

The ship docks at a quay in Buenos Aires. In the daytime not one dock worker is to be found. Towards evening they turn up one after another. Swim notices that they are all very neatly dressed. Though they are just dock workers, they are all wearing overcoats, and suits underneath, and neckties. Their manners are mild, and they never really raise their voices. It is only after they get to the pier that they change into their work clothes.

There are trucks on the quay. The cargo crane lifts half a ton of fertilizer and puts it on a truck, then repeats the routine. The ship's first mate has suddenly become very busy; he is standing on deck supervising the unloading of the cargo. The second mate is also busy; he follows the first mate around, pointing at this and that, walking to and fro like the pendulum of a clock. The third mate is also busy. There are forty-eight of us on board, and he is responsible for checking our numbers. Those whose passports are due to expire have to be registered; then a doctor will come on board, and everyone must have a medical. As soon as the ship docks, people who normally have very little to do have all come out.

Swim has nothing to do now, and he is standing in the midst of other similarly unoccupied people, waiting to go ashore. The Customs officials are also here, and Swim is given a shore permit after he has pressed the prints of ten fingers on a sheet of paper. Isn't it just the thumb? How come it's ten fingers here? Argentina is really a strange country. Perhaps the Argentines all like collecting fingerprints, thinks Swim. Now Swim's feet are on *terra firma*, which is a really nice feeling.

Liberty has always been fond of walking along Fat Sha Tsui. She likes window shopping. Whatever shop it is, she will stand outside and take a good look at the display windows, and she would like to know as much as possible about the things in the shop. If it is a florist's, say, Liberty would like to know how the dried flowers can be so dry and yet so healthy.

There are always lots of things in the shops. Some are huge, some tiny. These are enough to occupy Liberty for several hours every Sunday afternoon. Sometimes Liberty comes here with Braids. As the two of them eat their ice lollies and look at the shops, Braids asks Liberty:

— will you still be eating ice lollies

— when you're sixty

When they walk past a playground, Braids goes and sits down on a swing, and Liberty sits down on another swing. And so they sit there, swinging back and forth, having a wonderful time. And then Braids asks Liberty all of a sudden:

— will you still be sitting on a swing

— when you're sixty

After this they walk along a passageway in a high-rise building. They have come up on the escalator, and after pushing open a glass door, they are inside the building. They will soon see a shop filled with antiques — all the desks, screens, lamps are obviously very old. Liberty feels that these cabinets, chests, corner tables and other things are filled with legend and history. All the tables, chairs, cabinets and stools gathered here look as though they are soundly asleep and will not wake up for a very long time. Liberty will then ask Braids:

— will you still want my company

— when I'm sixty

— will you still have time for me

— when I'm sixty

Liberty likes the big medicine chest with over a hundred drawers in the antique shop. Every drawer has the name of a herb written on it: fritillery bulbs, loquat leaves, schisandra, petasites and cynanchum. These are names of flowers, grasses and leaves. Liberty cannot smell any herbal scent. This strange chest, where has it come from?

Next to the antique shop is a florist. On this day, all the flowers in the shop are different shades of the same colour: pink, pale red, light red, purplish red. It seems that the shop is filled with water lilies and peach blossoms. That is why Braids says that the shop looks just like a huge strawberry cream cake.

On this side of the display window there is a big vase. Braids says that this vase looks like a container for distilled water. However, there is no water in the vase now, instead there are various tiny plants. It is a glass garden, says Braids. The vase has a tiny neck not even big enough for an egg to go through, and yet its body is fat, like a water boiler. The plants inside are growing in a thin layer of soil. From the greenness of their leaves one can see they are growing healthily.

— what will happen

— when the leaves grow big

asks Braids.

Liberty is unable to answer the question. Tomorrow is a heavy burden. At this moment, the world in the vase is peaceful and serene. The delicate plants are absolutely still; they look as if they will never sprout one more leaf, as if they will never grow any taller, not even by one millimetre.

Next to the florist is a toy shop. On this day, besides the usual teddy bears, stringed puppets, Lego and complex jigsaw puzzles, there are two best-selling toys on display. One is a rubbish bug complete with four toes and a bodyful of spots. The other is a white blur of a ghost.

The toy shop holds an annual monster competition. The result this year has been computed and is now written on a board. Liberty remembers what was written on the board last year: You don't play mahjongg; you are a monster. Liberty recalls that there were similar words on the board the year before that: You don't read the animal press; you are a monster. Now, Liberty sees these words on the board:

you compose modern poetry

you are a monster

Next to the toy shop is an English bookshop. This shop likes to display fresh books in eye-catching positions, as if they are newly baked bread, so that everyone can smell the sweetness of heat, butter, eggs and sugar between the pages and conjure up rows and rows of jam rolls, crisply baked on the outside, white and soft and oozing with jam on the inside. Fresh books are like fresh bread: when they are displayed in a good spot in the window, their faces become the focal point of many eyes.

There is a large number of novels in the bookshop; they are the apple series. All the detective novels have a green apple printed on the covers; all the romance novels have blue apples; as for the best sellers, they have gold apples. Since there are many apple buyers, only very few gold apples are left.

Recently, the apple novels publishing company has launched a new product which has taken them many years of experimentation to develop. It is called instant novels. What is special about it is that the novel is treated and reduced to canned concentrates, like milk powder. The reader need only take one of the cans home, dilute the powder in boiling water as you would with instant coffee, and drink it up. Those who drink instant novels will see scene after scene from the novel appearing in their mind, just like a film.

The apple instant novel heralds a new era in the novel industry. With such advantages as being not harmful to the eyes and making no demands that anyone should know Chinese, English, French, German or Russian, it is of course doing excellently. According to those who have tried the instant novels, detective ones taste slightly bitter; romance ones come in two flavours, one sour as lemon and the other sweet and insubstantial as cotton candy.

And what do the critics say about instant novels? One of them is of this opinion: In this day and age, few of us have time for long screeds and brain-taxing works. We should provide readers with easily digestible spiritual nourishment which is high in entertainment value, agreeable, and time-saving. For this reason, the apple instant novels are a great invention.

16

This round: dogs

Today we have been out repairing telephones again. We stood in front of an iron gate and rang the bell, when all of a sudden a dog inside started barking fiercely. A man opened the door and looked at us cross-eyed from behind an iron chain. We asked him: Did you file a report saying that your telephone is out of order? We are here to repair it. At which point Merry Mak showed his identification card.

The crossed-eye man unlatched the chain, opened the door and pulled opened the gate with a loud clatter. A huge black dog with a face like a wash basin was standing at the door, barking fiercely again. We stood outside the door, pointing at the bad-tempered rascal. The owner of the dog said: It doesn't bite; it's a good dog. Come on in. And so we went in.

Merry Mak was the first to walk in. As soon as he set foot in the house, the bad-tempered dog walked round him and sniffed him once, twice, three times. Suddenly it opened its jaws wide and bit ferociously. Merry Mak started howling while his leg started bleeding.

At this point the dog owner quickly pulled the dog to one side and tied it up. He then brought out some liniment. Merry Mak rolled up his trousers to reveal two tooth holes in his leg. The dog owner poured liniment on the wound, and the blood mingled freely with the liniment.

— I need to see a doctor
— your telephone will have to wait

Merry Mak said. We picked up our bags, swung them across our shoulders and ran out of the house. We heard the dog owner closing the iron gate with a loud clatter and then banging his door shut. We hastily caught a taxi and made our way to the company doctor's clinic. The doctor bathed Merry Mak's wound and put medication on it, while saying over and over that it was best to have a check-up in hospital. He then wrote a letter, signed it, and handed it to Merry Mak. And so after ten minutes we arrived at the hospital's emergency unit.

Merry Mak handed the letter to a man in the office. The man asked Merry Mak for his name, address, and also asked what the problem was. Merry Mak said: Got bitten by a dog.

The emergency unit was very full that day. The benches in the lobby were filled with people. Every patient who had come here was accompanied by at least four or five relatives and friends. Since there was such a crowd, we sat down and waited. It turned out that the two sitting in front of us were there because they had had a fight. Their eyes and noses were all swollen, and their bodies were patches of red and purple.

Two people held their heads in their hands: they had headaches. One man who was throwing up was admitted into the treatment room at once. At regular intervals we could hear the noise of cars outside, then a group of people walked in, clamouring; this happened almost once every two minutes. Now someone was carried in by several people, the patient's face was the colour of stone. Now it was a father carrying a baby who was breathing only faintly. Then there was this young woman who walked in with one hand wrapped in a thick towel; she said that while chopping up a chicken she had chopped off a finger by mistake.

Compared with these people, Merry Mak could hardly be considered an emergency case. However, after we had waited for some time, his turn came. We went into the treatment room together. It was a spacious room divided by white screens into seven or eight smaller cubicles. Looking at these cloth-partitioned units I was suddenly reminded of changing rooms at the beaches.

The treatment room smelled of medicine and antiseptic, a smell peculiar to hospitals which reminds you of wounds and flowers. We had said earlier that day that we'd go swimming after work, but now we had ended up here, quite unexpectedly.

The doctor on duty took a brief look at Merry Mak's wound which had been dressed; now there was a faint trace of yellow left by the medication. This doctor also took some ointment out to put on Merry Mak's wound, after which he said to Merry Mak:

— would you like an injection

— would you like anti-rabies medication

he asked. Normally when Merry Mak goes to see a doctor, it is always the doctor who makes the decisions. When the doctor says: Injection, the nurse comes in with needle and syringe. When Merry Mak is ill and goes to the doctor, he is exactly like a lamb. And yet now this doctor was saying: You have to make up your own mind.

The doctor explained that with dog bites there are two possibilities: you either get rabies, or you don't. Whether you do depends entirely on whether the dog that bit you had rabies or not. The person who gets bitten should take one of the following courses of action immediately:

1. As a preventive measure, be inoculated with anti-rabies injections

2. Take the dog for examination

Now it occurred to Merry Mak he had been told by a friend that anti-rabies injections are horrible things. He was told that the needles are extra thick and extra long, and you had to have a series of twenty-four injections, and the needle goes in through your navel every time.

Merry Mak asked me what he should do. I said: The dog didn't look like it was mad with rabies, it was probably just bad-tempered, so perhaps we can ask it to come for a check-up. And so Merry Mak told the doctor he would opt for the second course of action. The doctor asked him to sign a form specifying that it was his choice not to have the anti-rabies injection. When we said goodbye to the doctor, he told us: You can't go to get the dog yourselves. You'd better report the case to the police. And so we did.

A policeman came with us to catch the dog. The crossed-eyed man pulled his iron gate open with a loud clatter. This time he had tied his dog up first and had given it a sound scolding, so it kept very quiet. When he learned that we had come to take the dog for an examination, he put a muzzle round its mouth and led it down the stairs with us, berating it as we walked: I thought you would be a good dog, I thought you would be a friend to humans, and now after I have kept you for all these years you bite a man. You beast, see if I don't serve you up for dinner tomorrow.

Though the dog had a muzzle on, it was still grumbling ferociously as it walked: I'm a loyal dog and I guard the house well, and look how you're treating me. See if I don't complain to the RSPCA.

This round: 709

Merry Mak has been transferred to 709. 709 is a department in the telephone company, and it is responsible for handling complaints. This has obviously affected Merry Mak's working hours. He no longer reports for duty at the exchange at eight in the morning, and he no longer leaves work at five in the afternoon. He is now working shifts. There are three shifts: morning, afternoon, and night. Sometimes he finishes work at midnight, and sometimes he is on the night shift and goes home at dawn.

Merry Mak did go to the hospital for one injection, but that was just normal medication. He said that it was probably for tetanus, but someone else said it was probably an antitoxin. The dog's medical examination revealed that it was a perfectly healthy, but rather unhappy, dog. That meant Merry Mak would not catch rabies. Though that was the case, Merry Mak still had to have three injections; the first two at three-month intervals, the last one six months after that.

In 709, Merry Mak sits in front of a machine every day, looking at the light signals, pressing buttons, listening to complaints. When someone says: My telephone is out of order, my number is such and such, and the telephone is wrong in this way or that, Merry Mak records the telephone number and passes it on to repairs.

Merry Mak receives a large number of such complaints every day. He says to himself: This isn't a particularly pleasant job; I never get any good news. He feels like the man sitting in the office of the hospital emergency unit; all he sees are ill and unhappy faces. The voices which come over the phone are always unhappy, either upset and angry, or nagging. So many telephones are out of order every day, what does that mean, thinks Merry Mak. It must be that communication between people is obstructed by a lot of external factors.

The job of listening to complaints is of course not as interesting as listening to music. Sometimes someone picks up the phone's ear piece and sends four-letter-words down the line. Sometimes someone says: This is a recession and everyone is hard up. You are a public utilities company, you should cut your prices.

There is nothing Merry Mak can do about these complaints. He can't say: I'm sorry, we only take care of complaints about out-of-order telephones, we are not the Consumer Council, and we are not the letters-to-the-editor column in a newspaper. Once Merry Mak actually said to one loud nagging voice: I agree completely with you that the phone company should cut its prices. Do you think I get a phone at home for free?

There is simply no end to the strange telephone calls. Someone asked: Who is your general manager today? And some people called to ask: What time is it? Others ask: It's raining so heavily, and there's thunder and lightning, has the Education Department made any announcements about suspending school today? People ask all these questions and more of the same, which have absolutely nothing to do with telephone repairs — questions about the weather report and beach signals for swimmers — you'd think that 709 is a special information station. However, Merry Mak does not object to being asked these questions. If he knows the answer, he always supplies it gladly.

There was this time when something strange happened at 709. A television station suddenly decided to hold a competition offering fabulous prizes. The whole population in the city was entitled to enter; all they had to do was get through on the phone. When evening came and the programme was aired, as soon as the competition questions were announced, Merry Mak saw every single light on all the machines in front of him suddenly come on, blazing like a beautiful Christmas tree. Merry Mak had never seen so many lights come on at the same time; he thought that 709 was having a firework display.

— put me through to the television station

— how come I can't get through

everyone was clamouring. That evening, because so many people were dialling the same number at the same time, the main telephone exchange became so overloaded that the machine broke down. This is really a strange city. Merry Mak recalled that some years ago, many people had used a similar method to stage a bank run, pushing the bank to total collapse. This is indeed a strange city.

This round: main street

Merry Mak went to work at four this afternoon, so when the time comes for him to go home, it is already midnight. Midnight is of course very late in the day; the streets are dark, the sky even darker. Though the lighting curfew[1] has been recently lifted, the sky is still very dark. No matter how many lighting displays there are, they cannot light up the sky.

At midnight, all the shops in the street are shut. This is a main street, so there are no food stalls, no small shops with half-open doors. Merry Mak looks around and sees that dark hollows of doors line both sides of the street; everyone is in hiding. The bustling crowds walking here in the daytime have disappeared. Occasionally a bus drives by, illuminated by yellowish lights inside. It is only at such moments that buses look exceptionally transparent.

After he gets off work at 709, Merry Mak goes home by minibus. He has to walk a short distance to catch a minibus, and when the minibus drops him in his neighbourhood, he has to walk the rest of the way home.

---

[1] As a result of the oil crisis in the 1970s, the government imposed a time limit on non-essential lighting such as advertisements and shop displays.

In the old days the main street used to be crowded even at night. There were people coming out of the cinemas, and people taking a stroll, but now all these people have disappeared. It is as though they all need to hibernate. Even Merry Mak quickens his steps as he walks down the main street, hoping to get home as soon as possible.

Merry Mak is not the only one to hurry home from 709. He usually walks down as far as the crossroads with a group of four or five. But by the time he is on the minibus, approaching his neighbourhood, Merry Mak is on his own. Sometimes Merry Mak comes across a policeman in the street.

— who are you

— what are you doing

The police always ask. Merry Mak stands still, takes out his staff ID card and shows it to the police. On this day, Merry Mak has not met any policeman. When he gets off the minibus and turns into a side street, three men walk up to him. They come face to face with Merry Mak, pause briefly, and then surround him. One of them says:

— we sworn brothers

— have run out of pocket money

All three fellows are heavily built. Since there is no one in the street, it would probably be futile to call out for help, Merry Mak figures. Even if someone were to pass by, it would be unlikely for him to be of any help, Merry Mak figures again. Merry Mak came across a policeman the night before. Will he meet another one tonight? No, no policeman comes round. It's always like this, Merry Mak says to himself, when you want to see the police, they never come; when you don't want to see them, they're always there. Now the three men standing around him all take a step towards him. Merry Mak takes all the money out of his pocket and hands it over to the man facing him. The man takes the money and points at Merry Mak's watch. There is nothing he can do except take it off. The watch shows the day of the month: twenty-third. Twenty-third. Well, this month I won't have enough money for meals and transport. And on Saturday I won't be able to go to the cinema. It seems to Merry Mak that his money and watch have sprouted ten wings.

— is that all you've got

the man facing Merry Mak says coldly. Merry Mak shakes his head. There's nothing left. I've given you everything, he says. While he is still shaking his head, a fist appears in front of his eyes. The fist blackens one of his eyes and makes him extremely giddy. Before Merry Mak can make up his mind what to do, he is hit twice on the stomach. He bends down and puts his arms around his belly. After a while, it is his back which feels the pain, and he puts his hand on his back. By the time Merry Mak opens his eyes and stands up, the people who were standing there have disappeared. The street is very dark; a white dog is standing beside some cardboard boxes, looking vacantly at him.

— how come it's you again

— did you get bitten by a dog again

the doctor at the emergency unit asks. It is the same doctor whom Merry Mak saw a few days before. This time Merry Mak is admitted into hospital. He has to spend a whole week there.

709 never sees Merry Mak back at work again. There is a note on the desk on which he has written: I have joined the city police force.

This round: countryside

We are planting telephone poles in the countryside. I am with a group of strangers. We carried heavy metal poles onto our vehicle and then came to the countryside to plant them in the ground one by one. Although it is hard and exhausting work, I like planting telephone poles. It feels like planting trees.

There are no telephone poles in the city streets; in the city, telephone wires all go underground. Telephone poles are only found in the countryside, in remote areas. When we go out to the countryside to plant telephone poles, we set off early in the morning and do not get back until late afternoon. Planting poles is group work. Three or four people are needed to carry one pole up a hill, and sometimes we have to cross a stream, it's all very lively.

Working up in the hills like that makes me feel like we are lumber-jacks. When a tree trunk has been sawn through, they all shout: T-i-m-b-e-r. And so a tree which has been standing proudly bends at the waist and falls down to one side, like a falling mountain.

We do not fell anything; we plant. We do not destroy; we build. In the hills and fields we plant row after row of mechanical trees. These trees are green, too, stretching out eight or ten string-shaped leaves. These trees bring distant voices of the outside world to remote villages.

I like these new trees growing in the countryside; I can spot them from a long way off. They are unlike electricity poles; those are grey, like the lampposts in the city. Telephone poles are green, like leafy vegetables in the field, like trees on the hills, like grass in the valley.

First, we dig a deep hole in the ground, and then we pull the pole up to a vertical position, and then we plant it in the hole. Like the lumber-jacks, we also shout; their shout is "timber", ours "up". We get sand and water to mix with the cement we have brought along, and then we pour the concrete mix into the empty space around the pole. When the mixture solidifies, the telephone pole has taken root in the ground.

After the telephone poles have been made to stand upright one by one, they are painted a dark green colour, and then linked together by electricity wires. Sometimes birds come to rest on the wires; sometimes a stray kite or two hang on the wires. Some stalks of ripened rice in the field stare with their golden eyes and say:

— these modern scarecrows

— how tall they are

On rainy days we continue planting telephone poles on a grassy slope. Sometimes when it rains really hard and flood water erodes the earth, we take shelter in a farmer's house for a while. The farming family will serve us tea in big rustic bowls with beautiful blue patterns.

I might take out a letter stuffed in my trouser pocket and read it. The stamps on the envelope are strange and novel, and in the letter Swim tells me about the Red Sea and the city of Jeddah.

At five in the afternoon the ship sailed into the Red Sea. Now I understand why it is called the Red Sea — at sunset, the whole sea looks red. There are many coral reefs in the Red Sea's shallow waters. According to the navigational chart this is an area where ships easily run aground, so we should drop anchor at night time.

The city of Jeddah is built by the sea, with its back to the desert. When the ship sails along the coastline, we can see mountains. The water vapour in mid-air displays a mirage of moving vehicles. It is very hot. The people here are Muslims and all alcoholic drinks are banned. The Customs people have sealed up the liquor cabinet on board our ship.

We have carried a cargo of sugar here. The cargo is lifted onto the quay by the crane on board, five packs at a time, each pack weighing 135 pounds. The work progresses slowly. There are no cranes on the quay, and the cargo is carried by men. Each man shoulders one pack of sugar and puts it onto a truck. The trucks are all very old.

The workers come to report for work at the pier at seven in the morning, but they do not actually start working until nine. At eight in the morning, at four in the afternoon, at sunrise and at sunset, the people of Jeddah put aside whatever work they may be engaged in, kneel down facing east and prostrate themselves on the ground, praying. They bow to the heavens like this every day.

This place is scorching hot at noon and cold at night. The women all have their faces covered. There are no cinemas, no sports ground, no street lamps. All the streets are mud tracks; the suburb is the desert. The buses bound for the countryside are painted green and yellow, with baggage racks on the top. I have not been on the buses; I ride a camel instead. When you ride a camel you sit on its neck, and the single-humped ones are really difficult for the rider. The camels have a sour smell, and the bad-tempered ones bite. We all wrap three huge pieces of cloth round ourselves. I have wrapped a red one round my body, a white one round my head, and a blue one round my neck and hands. Bells dangle from the camels' necks, and the mats we sit on are like carpets, fully embroidered, with fluffy balls of wool hanging down the fringes.

In this place you can carry as much money around as you like. No one would steal from you or rob you. The penalty for stealing or robbing money: Amputation of the hands.

The upper reaches of the Suez Canal were bombed, with the result that a score of ships were sunk or ran aground on the Canal. At high tide you can see the masts; at low tide you can see the thick rust on the bodies of the ships. War has left its mark of ownership on these vessels.

— and how is my city
Swim asks.

This round: machines
— when you take the phone apart
— can you put it back together
the engineer asks.
— when you pull the wires apart
— can you re-connect them
the engineer asks.

At regular intervals, the engineer comes to ask us what we have learned. He comes to test our knowledge of telephones, to see what level we are at. Sometimes he gives us more knowledge, sometimes he decides whether to send us to attend classes at Lily Pond or not.

Running around the city repairing telephones is about learning technique; attending classes at Lily Pond is about learning theory. To take apart a telephone and to link up a severed wire is technique; to understand why a severed wire means a dead phone or a babbling phone, and why when it is properly linked up there are no unwanted noises is theory. At the moment, I have more telephone techniques than theories.

I only have to pick up the handset and twist the earpiece, and a small disc comes off. You can see three holes in the earpiece, and when the disc comes off, you can see a piece of stainless metal inside, with the same three holes in it. This piece of metal can be taken out, revealing one red and one green wire at the back. Both wires are connected to the mouth-piece through the hollow handle.

I twist the mouthpiece, and another disc comes off. The cross-section of the mouthpiece looks like a diagram of bacteria: it is full of holes of various sizes. Under the piece of metal are compressed granules of carbon.

— if there is a noise when you shake it

— the phone is out of order

I say. The engineer nods in approval.

I have now taken the metal piece off, and under it lie two wires, one white and one blue. They join the red and green wires coming down from the earpiece making four wires, all of which run through loops of hair-ringlet-like wire into the telephone.

The telephones are now made of soft plastic. In the old days it used to be hard plastic, which was very heavy. I detach two screws from the cradle of the handset, and the telephone set is divided into two halves. There is a wire diagram on the upper half which specifies which wire goes where, and what colours they are. I don't have to look at it, however, because I know precisely which wire should go round which terminal.

There are only a few things inside a telephone. Two brass bells in the front, with a brass rod in the middle linked to a bundle of wrapped brass wire. When someone gets through on the phone, the wires are connected, and the brass stick strikes the bells. This sound is very precise: *d-i-n-g*, *d-i-n-g*.

The screws on the bell can also be taken off. When the two bells are put close together, the ringing is not so loud; the further apart they are, the louder the ringing.

In the telephone there is also a wooden box, a brass seat supporting the handset, and a basic combination dial. I loosen a screw and take the dial off. I'd better give the dial a clean-up since so much dust has gathered on it. And so I detach the small disc in the middle of the dial, the piece of paper under the disc, the screw under the paper, the two screws on either side, and the spring between the two screws.

And so the round piece of plastic with numbers written on it parts company with its friends. I wipe them clean very thoroughly. There are many things lying behind the dial: cogs and a wheel. There is also a spring. When a number is dialled and the wheel reverts to its original position, the spring vibrates *tick tick tick tick*, and the machine at the exchange gets the message. If it's seven numbers, the spring vibrates seven times.

What the engineer wants to find out is whether I actually know how to connect the circuits or not. When he sees that I have taken the phone apart and detached all sorts of irrelevant screws, discs and springs, he says: take the coloured wires apart, and I do as he says.

At the tail end of the telephone set there is a bunch of coloured wires all connected to U-shaped tabs. There are two neat rows of terminals on the set: one to nine, and ten to nineteen; nineteen terminals altogether. The wires are really colourful. Besides the red, green, white and blue ones from the handset, there is a set of five consisting of brown, grey, blue, pink and orange. And so I unscrew every single one of them, mix them all up, and then put them back in the right position one by one.

And then I return the dial section and the handset section to their original form. As I take the telephone apart and then put it back together, I think that the phone is really a fascinating machine. Just a few pieces of brass, some plastic and some wires, but put them together, and they actually speak.

As I work on the telephone, I am suddenly reminded of human beings. Humans are in fact strange, fascinating talking machines. It is said that a man who weighs 150 pounds consists of 3500 cubic feet of gases: oxygen, hydrogen and nitrogen. The twenty-two pounds and ten ounces of carbon in the body makes enough lead for 9000 pencils. The blood in the human body contains fifty grains of iron (one grain is equal to 0.0648 metric grammes, or gm. for short). Together with the iron in other parts of the body, it is enough to make a nail large enough to support your own body weight, so you can nail yourself to the wall.

The fifty ounces of phosphate in the human body are enough for making 800,000 matchheads. The human body also contains sixty sugar cubes, twenty teaspoonfuls of salt, thirty-eight quarts of water, two ounces of chalk. There are also carbohydrates, sulphur, hydrogen, magnesium, and hydrochloric acid. All this, put together, turns the human being into a strange talking machine.

I put the telephone back together. I dial a number, and the telephone rings normally and regularly. The engineer nods in approval.

— go to Lily Pond for classes

— a week from now

he says.

Oh, well, that means I'll have to sit looking at a blackboard again.

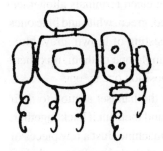 

17

On this day, a large number of people in the square are looking up at a building which looks like a Greek temple. There is a statue of a goddess at the top of the building, holding a set of scales in her hand. These people are looking at the building and pointing their fingers at the statue because the set of scales has inexplicably disappeared.

Someone expresses his opinion on this incident. He says: The set of scales has been taken off to be replaced because the city is now changing to the metric system. Those who hear this all say: So that's why. They disperse, and then spread the news, telling everyone that it's because of this that that happened.

A man who lives on the top floor of a building returned to his flat at around four that morning, carrying a big paper bag. When he opened the bag, there was a set of scales inside. He looked at the scales for a while, didn't use them to measure anything, just hung them up on a nail in the wall.

— these may come in useful
he said.
— hope they aren't too inaccurate
he said.

The flat that this person lives in is not partitioned into living and sleeping areas. You can see the contents of the whole flat wrapped between four walls. There is paper everywhere, piled up taller than a man.

The man has no bed. When he is tired he

sleeps on a pile of paper. When he is awake, he reads these sheets of paper from morning to night. There are words written on the sheets: some words form a poem, others an essay, yet others a story. The man who sleeps on paper reads these poems, essays and stories every day.

In this flat, besides the paper which is littered everywhere, there are also rulers everywhere. These rulers look very similar, but when you use them to measure things, you will find that they are very different.

This man who lives on the top floor is very old, and because he is very old, his hair has turned grey. Though his hair is grey, he is still in robust health. He believes that he can climb to the top of Sleeping Lion Rock and look at the view. This man has retired now. With his pension, he bought this flat. He also has a monthly allowance and some money put by over the years. He does not have to worry about making a living.

This man actually has a daughter and two sons. When they graduated from secondary school, he sent them to universities overseas. The result is: none of them wants to come back. Sometimes they send photographs, sometimes Father's Day cards, asking after him: Father, how are you?

This man living on the top floor is fine. When other people's hair turns as grey as his, they say: Should I get a bowl of fish to pass the time? Should I grow some flowers to eliminate time? He never asks himself these questions. He does not care for fish and he grows no flowers. He just reads the sheets of paper in his flat from morning to night, so absorbed in them that he sometimes forgets about meals; he also forgets the twice-yearly medical at the doctor's.

Sometimes he goes out in search of paper in the streets. Are there any papers worth reading? he asks. If there are, he carries them home. Even when they aren't any good, he still carries them home to find out why they are no good.

When he goes out, he occasionally walks past a park, and he'll go in and walk around. There are always grey-haired ones sitting in the park, staring vacantly at nothing. So lonely, the grey-haired say. He walks briskly by. Lonely? He has no time for that. He is busy looking for paper to bury his head in.

When he goes out looking for paper, he also looks for rulers. He is always saying: I have to find an accurate ruler. For many years now he has been searching for the ideal ruler. Rulers are many, but they are all slightly faulty in one way or another.

And so though the rulers in his flat form a pile that almost reaches the ceiling, he is still looking.

This man who lives on the top floor likes to measure paper with his rulers. Whenever he finishes a sheet or a pile, he measures it. He will tell his rulers that this is a long story covering many generations, and the rulers will measure it generation by generation and give a detailed account of the family history of various characters in the story. Sometimes the paper tells stories about many countries, covering a dozen cities, and the rulers will carefully distinguish between the various countries and cities.

The rulers all look the same, but they are in fact all different. When they measure paper, their individual personalities become apparent.

Take this instance: once, after the man had finished reading a pile of paper, he took out the rulers to measure it. He took out many rulers because he was aware of their fondness for opinionating. He knew that rulers are not used to keeping quiet. One ruler said: In this pile it describes people sprouting wings and taking off to the moon; it is Surrealism.

Another ruler said: Obviously it's space ships shuttling through space; it is science fiction. Yet another ruler said: Cutting a hole in a garment; it's obviously Dadaism. And another ruler said: Sealing ID cards in plastic, what else is it if not Neo-Realism? Some other rulers continue with their commentaries: Talking about so many ants and bees is Naturalism; planting flowers on the beach is Existentialism, etc.

The man who lives on the top floor watched the rulers carry out their measurements for a good part of the day only to come up with so many -isms; he shook his head. He picked up the rulers and threw them in a corner of the room. The pile of rulers continued to express their measured views.

They said: It keeps talking about a teapot and doesn't mention any humans. Since it is more concerned about a teapot than about people, it's an anti-novel. And then they said: This man's thoughts turn suddenly to a tree in the street, suddenly to a chair in the house, it's Stream of Consciousness. They also said: All these idioms can be grouped together. Idioms are ready-made products; we can send these ready-made products to an exhibition. And then they said: If it opens its mouth to talk and you see colourful words the shape of flowers, it is Magic Realism. And then they said: No beginning and no ending, singing and screaming at will, it must be a happening.

One particular ruler in a corner of the room kept extremely quiet. This ruler prides itself on being the World Authority Ruler. It is said that this ruler had once measured a pile of World No. 1 paper, and since then it has been calling itself the World Authority Ruler. Since it became World Authority, it has steadfastly refused to measure any other paper because to do so, it thinks, would be inconsistent with its status. And so this ruler stands in a corner of the room, keeping very quiet no matter what the other rulers say. Whenever the man who lives on the top floor sees this ruler, he says: Since you refuse to measure paper, you are no longer a ruler. You're World No. 1 rubbish.

There are other rulers which were at the bottom of the pile and seldom had the chance of being taken out to measure paper, and so their chances of expressing their opinions were limited. However, this did not silence them; they were screaming in the corner of the room all the same. One of them shouted: There must be a native flavour, a flavour of mud, of straw huts, of ducks. Then another ruler shouted: There must be a city flavour, a flavour of steel, of plastic, of electricity wires. Yet another ruler shouted: There must be social consciousness, in the form of faces, ears, fingers, and toes. Still another ruler said there should be a long range missile. The one clamouring for a missile was a metal tape measure.

The man living on the top floor just let the rulers chatter on. He said to himself: Far better to talk to the paper, and so he sat down on a pile of paper, picked one sheet up at random, and started reading.

— how are you

he said.

— fine, thank you

said the sheet of paper.

— please don't measure me with those rulers

— please don't measure me with those rulers

said the paper.

The man living on the top floor nodded in agreement. In the pile of paper he was reading there were the following people: one Fruits, who likes singing bake some bread bake some bread it sure tastes good; one Braids, who lives with an alarm clock; one Liberty, who has drawn a hippo with four toes; one Silly, who knows where to find pineapples; one Merry Mak, who has red chilies hanging all over his walls; and one North, who knows how to make really good doors.

The man read and chatted to the pieces of paper.

— what is your name

he asked.

— I'm Nonsense

the paper replied.

At this point, some of the rulers saw that their owner was busy reading sheets of paper. They became very excited at the sight of this. We'll get paper to measure soon, they shouted. Shoving and pushing, they squeezed themselves in front of the pile of paper.

When the owner of the flat finished reading one sheet, the rulers thought that he would pick them up to measure it with. Yet when the flat owner put down the sheet he was holding, it was just to pick up another sheet. In this way, four hours passed. The rulers naturally became very impatient. After another long while, the flat owner was still reading the pile of paper.

As the rulers had nothing to do, they too craned their necks to look at the paper. After a while, they naturally formed their opinions. A curving ruler was the first to speak up: I have no idea what this pile is trying to say. The story line is non-existent, characterization is messy, incidents are disconnected, the structure is loose. A section here and a section there, it's just like old newspaper the pork seller uses to wrap up the meat. As it said so, it yawned.

An exceptionally straight ruler shook both its ends for three minutes and said repeatedly: I am revolted by this; it is completely outside of my experience.

There is a triangular ruler, an asymmetrical triangle. It tried very hard to find various geometrical forms in the pile of paper. The result was that it did not find its own form, the triangle, nor did it find any other form, not the circle, not the rectangle, not the hexagon. It sighed. The T square next to it sighed as well.

The metal tape measure had now also forced its way to the front. It had a loud voice and so what it said could be heard over the clamour. It shouted: There must be something eternal, something lasting. And so it buried its head to look for this something in the pile. Seeing this, the man living on the top floor picked up a plastic flower and stuffed it into tape measure's mouth.

Some rulers stood there looking for a while and then turned their back on the pile. Who wants to read any of that! It seemed that everyone had cast their vote. The weather was so hot, they decided to go back for a nap in the corner of the flat. That is why after a short while, it looked as though many boiling kettles had been placed in that corner, all emitting countless ZZZ's.

The man living on the top floor had by now finished quite a number of pages. As he read, he marked the pages with a pencil. Frequently he took out the marked sections and asked Nonsense to explain.

— how did it begin

— what was the initial motivation

he asked.

— it was because

— I saw a pair of jeans

Nonsense replied.

It was like this. I saw a pair of jeans in the street. I saw that the person wearing that pair of jeans was also wearing a comfortable cotton shirt, and a pair of sneakers. He was carrying a simple cloth bag, going hiking.

It occurred to me that the way people live today is very different from the way they lived in the past; no more table-cloth-like skirts, no more stiffly starched long-sleeved white shirts. This city is also different from what it was before; no more Chinese drumming and piping in the streets, no more roads covered in the shadows of bicycles. That was the beginning.

Besides, there was the weather, fine weather. I saw the hair of the person wearing jeans: it was the colour of sunlight. The face was wine coloured, like a cooked lobster. I guess we had all walked out of the pale unhealthy shadow of those Nihilist and Existentialist black wings. That was the beginning.

The man living on the top floor sifted through some of the sheets and then pointed to a mark.

— here

— you mention *Tout va bien*

he said.

— that was the beginning

— I started talking nonsense in the *Tout va bien* manner

said Nonsense.

As for *Tout va bien*, it is like this. Nonsense likes *Tout va bien* because it sang this song: As long as the same old sun shines overhead, everything is fine. *Tout va bien* is a film. Its director is fond of collage techniques; he is also used to following the whole scene with the eye of the camera and taking in all the objects and action in one shot.

— I used a moving narrative

— and a series of collages

said Nonsense. The earthquake last night took place in Badan Village on the Kelakunlun Road thirty-four miles north of Tagete in Xinjiang. That is collage. Israel will not give up strategic Metulla and Ein Gedi, or the Abu Rudeis oil fields in Sinai. That, too, is collage.

The man living on the top floor does not object to ready-made products. Now he pulls out a pile of collages from a corner of the room, a few of which were also the work of the director of *Tout va bien*. He said: Look, these collages create new meaning and fun out of existing things, but your collage is just like a basket of newly dug up potatoes.

— here

— you mention *A Hundred Years of Solitude*

he said.

He went to another corner of the room and pulled out a few sheets of paper to show Nonsense. Look, these few pages are about the big-winged angel. The angel falls into a muddy pond; the angel is put into a chicken coop; the angel is surrounded by people looking at it as though it is a zoo animal. Finally the angel manages to fly away. It takes just a few pages, ten pages to be exact, to tell a good story. As for you, now it's a river that doesn't flow, now it's travelling to space and sending back a photo taken with a black hole, you keep babbling for over a hundred pages, and you keep chattering about this moral and that moral. That's adding legs to a snake. That's installing organs inside a doll. The fact is, you are not one who knows how to moralize. As he said so, he handed Nonsense a mirror.

And then he said to Nonsense, these pictures don't go with the text, that's because your arithmetic is bad and you made the wrong calculations. All these phrases are wrong, that's because your language ability is bad, and you don't know one phrase from another. He picked up a piece of paper at random; on the paper is written: "The Yellow Emperor of yore, ancestor of all Chinese, family name Gongsun, personal name Xuanyuan, was born with superhuman intelligence. As a baby the sire could talk; as a child the sire understood humility; as a youth the sire was reliable; as an adult the sire was perceptive." He told Nonsense to study these words carefully.

18

It is after lunch. For me, lunch time is around one in the afternoon, or one-thirty. If I eat quickly, I have more free time to do the things I like, things such as: strolling in the streets, window shopping, watching children play hopscotch. I am not strolling in the streets today, however, because there are no streets here. I am in the countryside, and there is nothing here except grass. Recently, our team has been planting telephone poles here. The sound of hello hello will soon reach this deserted place.

Just now I had my lunch on the grassy slope. I had brought my own lunch box containing a spicy salted drumstick, a hot dog and sandwiches. I also brought some soft drinks. I finished everything. I sat alone on the grass and had my lunch. This morning, six of us came out to this place together. A few days ago, we planted countless telephone poles here. Yesterday, we painted them all a dark green, and we linked up all the relevant wires. Today, we are here to see if the telephones work here. This is the final phase of our job.

Four of the people who came here with me have gone on to even more remote parts to install telephone lines and telephone sets, leaving only me and my team-mate on this grassy area. After standing under the sun for a while this team-mate friend of mine suddenly had a headache; his face turned pale, and sweat ran down his forehead. It was probably sunstroke. After resting under

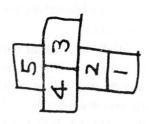

a tree for a while, his breathing returned to normal, and he went to catch a bus to return to the city.

And so I am the only one left on this grassy slope. If this were Fat Sha Tsui, I'd probably be looking at cars in the air-conditioned walkways of commercial buildings, thinking how convenient it would be to go swimming in the countryside if I had a motorized bicycle. Or I would be looking at records in a shop window, thinking about buying a record player on hire purchase — or should I save enough money for it first?

Right now I am not in Fat Sha Tsui, I am sitting in a grassy area in the countryside. The weather today is extremely respectable; the sky has carefully tinted its face with the colour of the sea. Such nice weather, such cool shade under the tree, perhaps I should take a nap here lying on the grass. And so I proceed. I use the canvas bag as my pillow. As I am sleeping on my side, a blade of grass stands right next to my mouth, and so I start chewing on it. I suppose I might just train myself to be an ox. It is said that on some grassland there are flowers with tiny petals, called daisies, decorating the clumps of grass, but here I don't see any. In Fat Sha Tsui there is this man squatting next to a black umbrella, making insects out of grass. Is it a grasshopper? A girl walking by says: It's a mantis. Another says it's a katydid. Yet another says perhaps it's a cricket.

I am of course not really asleep. I am just lying there, watching the sky busying itself: it has changed its way of tending its flock of sheep six times, and yet is still dissatisfied. While I am looking at the sky, and occasionally looking at the grass like this, a man has come to stand behind my head. He is a man with curly hair. I think that he may be an angel.

— am I disturbing you

he asks.

I tell him not at all, but that he has disturbed the grasshopper. And so he promises to find the grasshopper for me. I also tell him that he has disturbed the flock of sheep in the sky. On hearing this he laughs heartily. He says that since the weather is so hot, would I mind if he sat down in the shade and chatted with me for a while. I immediately agree to it. I have nothing to do right now, and I love chatting. He sits down.

— there are so many clouds in the sky

he says.

— what happens when the sky is crowded with clouds

— so crowded that there's not enough space for them

he asks.

I tell him that's simple: when the clouds are crowded they turn into waterdrops which form rain and fall on the earth.

— what happens when the earth is crowded with people

— so crowded that there's not enough space for them

he asks.

I tell him that's simple, too. When the earth is filled with people it will be packed full; every single centimetre will have people standing on it, and those who come late will have to stand on the heads of those already there, like building a stone wall, layer upon layer, until at last the earth will cry out: I can't hold you anymore! whereupon the force of gravity will give up on them, and the outermost layer of people all fall off into space, like fireworks, very nice to look at.

So that's it, he says. Does that mean you do not envisage any problems. I tell him that there will of course be no problems. The people looking like nice fireworks will fly off to other planets; they can become Martians, Uranians, Jupiterians, and Sunians.

The curly-haired one then asks me: Do you agree with the view that we should stop living? I shake my head to show I disagree. In that case what are you doing here? he asks. Actually I am also puzzled by his way of questioning me. And so I ask him back: What about you, what are *you* doing here?

— I've come to interview someone

he answers. He says he is a reporter.

— I've come to install telephone lines

I tell him, pointing at the row of telephone poles nearby. As the curly-haired reporter realizes that I am not the target of his interview, he stops chatting to me. He stands up and runs towards another grassy area where many people are walking to and fro. This man! Though I wasn't really asleep, his clatter drove away my grasshopper, and then he refused to chat to me.

I am now sitting on the horizontal bar on top of a telephone pole. I have been sitting here for quite a while. I am wearing a cap, and I am up here on the telephone pole to see how the phone lines are. In front of me there is a box containing wires which are linked to other telephone poles; now the wires have all been properly connected, and the ends are sealed in this box. As soon as the lines are installed, the telephones will work. I put an earpiece on to see if there is any sound.

There is no sound. It's very quiet here. Sitting on top of the telephone pole, I can see the distant mountains. On the other side of the grassy slope there is a small white house. Further away, there are some moving cars. In the most distant place, there is a city which looks as if it is on fire.

Under the telephone pole there is grass, green grass. The grass is of a fresh green colour, very healthy. If I could create the world all over again, what colour would I give to the grass? Red grass, that's too hot. Yellow grass, that would look like a wheat field. Blue grass, what about the sea then? There is really no other choice. It's best for the grass to be green.

There is now a cloud floating right above the peak of a big mountain. The mountain looks dark purple, the way mountains do in glaring sunlight. On the mountain ridge there are rows and rows of dense trees, which make the mountain look like a hedgehog. On the other side of the mountain, perhaps there is a little hut which has taken a whole spring to build. Moreover, it has a red roof, the same as fairy-tale huts. Moreover, there is a red-and-white chequered chair.

If I went and sat on that red-and-white chequered chair, what would I be doing? No, I won't be sleeping. No, my hands won't be holding a hot muffin. I may be eating a slice of water melon sitting on a chair like that, or I may be chewing a joint of sweet sugarcane. I think I'd be reading story books sitting in that chair. No, no, I think I'd be holding the handset of a telephone in my hand.

When I picked up the phone, I'd dial a number — to whom? I'd call home. Is Braids there? She has gone hiking with her classmates. She said she was going to catch crabs on the beach. She was going to build a fairy-tale castle on the sand. Is mother there? She must be out shopping in the market. Tonight I may get winter melon soup at dinner, and there'd be pieces of lotus leaves floating in the soup. Mother may decide to buy half a chicken, and there'd be sprigs of coriander on the chicken. Mother would buy Chinese spinach, cut off the roots, and stir fry it with garlic. Mother is always saying how a whole catty of vegetables ends up a pitifully small dish.

Would my aunt Liberty be home? She'd be at No. 1 Hobby Horse Road, reading. It has turned out that half of the books have been eaten by bookworms. When she took them down from the shelves, the pages looked like paper-cuttings. Because of that she stood there sighing for a good part of the day. She must be there, tidying up the books. North, the doorman has not been making doors for quite a while now. He has been knocking and hammering, and sanding wood, and painting it. He is making a puppet. A big doll for Braids, he says. I have no idea what kind of a puppet it is; I wonder if it will be a stringed puppet.

If I wanted to make a call, I could also call Merry Mak. I'd ask him: Are you happy with your work? I'd also ask him: How are your chilies? When I pick up the phone, I can even call up someone I do not know and say: How are you, whoever you are.

— whoever you are

— how are you

I say to the telephone handset.

— very well

— thank you

the telephone handset says to me. It is a strange voice, a muffled voice, a distant voice. I hear a voice; someone is talking to me. I am delighted to hear the voice coming from the other end of the line.

— hello, hello

I shout.

— verily I say to thee

— there is no need for you to worry

says the voice on the other end of the line.

— hello, hello

— who are you

I shout again.

— the earth is undergoing metabolism. The earth is producing its own next generation. The earth is a cell. It is a living creature. It will give birth to a new baby

— In the midst of icebergs in the southern pole, a mountain will rise up from the crust of the earth; an island will appear in the ocean: that will be our new earth

says the voice on the other end of the telephone.

— on this new planet, the mineral resources will be much richer than what we have now. The water in the ocean will be unpolluted by any chemicals. We will go to the new planet by ship; our ship will be the second Noah's Ark. The old earth will gradually wither away, like a snake shedding its skin, and it will be incinerated by volcanic fire. Human beings, having learned from their painful experience, will build a brave new world on this new planet

says the voice on the other side of the telephone line. I have no idea who is speaking on the other end; it sounds strange and distant. But I am delighted to hear that voice. There is a voice in the phone, that means the line has been connected, and my job is done. I look at my watch: five o'clock sharp. I knock off at five. So, goodbye. Goodbye, sun, goodbye. Goodbye, grass, goodbye.